Burpstronauts

by M. D. Payne

Grosset & Dunlap
An Imprint of Penguin Group (USA) LLC

To Francesco, for giving me the chance

GROSSET & DUNLAP
Published by the Penguin Group
Penguin Group (USA) LLC, 375 Hudson Street, New York, New York 10014, USA

USA | Canada | UK | Ireland | Australia | New Zealand | India | South Africa | China

penguin.com
A Penguin Random House Company

Library of Congress Cataloging-in-Publication Data is available.

ISBN 978-0-448-46229-5   10 9 8 7 6 5 4 3 2 1

Prologue

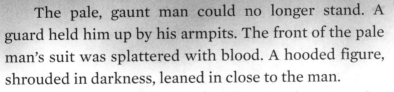

The pale, gaunt man could no longer stand. A guard held him up by his armpits. The front of the pale man's suit was splattered with blood. A hooded figure, shrouded in darkness, leaned in close to the man.

"Where. ISSSSS. IT?!" The hooded figure's voice boomed. "I will not ask again."

The pale man's words came out as a mumble. "It's somewhere safe." His teeth were stained with blood. "I can assure you of that."

"Safe? Soon *nowhere* will be safe," the hooded figure hissed. Black spittle shot out from the hood. "It's just a matter of time. Still, I would rather not wait." He leaned in closer. "Tell me where it is . . . and it would be best if you answered my question this time. You should be very afraid indeed if you force me to ask again."

"Show me your face," said the man calmly. "Then perhaps I shall answer your question."

The hooded figure pulled away and clutched his hood closer around his head.

"Who I am is of no consequence to you," he said, his voice growing loud with anger.

"It seems I'm not the only one suffering from fear," said the man. He laughed through his pain, showering blood deep into the hood of the figure.

"THE PENDANT!" yelled the hooded figure, his voice echoing around the massive throne room. "It shall be mine—no matter how hard you protest. I shall find a way into that feeble mind of yours and extract the answer. Where is the real pendant?"

The hooded figure held up a pendant, waving it in front of the pale, gaunt man's face. "How dare you try to trick me with this *fraud*!"

He then crushed the bloodstone like a corn puff from a sugary breakfast cereal. It turned to powder with a CRUNCH.

"How dare I?!" asked the man, still laughing. "I would have been insane to hold on to the power once I realized you sought it. Oh no, I put it somewhere you would never, EVER think to look, you insane, broken creature. How dare *you*? What are *you* of all people going to do with all eight pendants? You haven't the strength in you, Cord—"

The hooded figure cut off the pale, gaunt man with a gloved fist to his stomach.

"OOOOOOF!"

The man fell to the floor in pain, too out of breath to scream. The guard leaned down to pick him up, but the hooded figure waved him away.

"Never speak that name here," hissed the hooded figure.

When the man got his strength back, he stared into the terrible red eyes of the hooded figure, spat a wad of blood on the floor, and laughed so hard that dust began to fall from the ceiling of the throne room.

"So it *is* you!" said the man. "Ha-ha-ha!"

"ENOUGH! Another kiss from my latest creation will dry up your laughter and loosen your tongue," said the hooded figure. "Oh yes, it shall break your spirit . . ."

He clapped his hands together. The guards at the door backed away slightly as a small man in a white laboratory coat pushed a large tank into the room. Dark water sloshed around, spilling out of the tank.

The man calmly watched as the tank approached.

The hooded figure pulled a slimy black serpent out of the tank and slowly brought it toward the mouth of the man. The serpent crackled slightly with a pulse of electricity as it came closer.

"Not quite yet, my sweet zapeel," the hooded figure cooed. "Be patient."

Two guards moved to the man, one on either side. One lifted him up, and the other grabbed his mouth, forcing it open.

"Argggglllll," gurgled the pale man, more blood oozing down his chin. He was trying desperately to pull his tongue deeper into his mouth.

The mouth of the serpent opened to reveal sharklike rows of teeth.

The hooded figure leaned in and latched the disgusting creature onto the pale man's tongue.

"AAAAABLLLLLRRRRSHHHH," the pale man screamed.

The hooded figure let go of the zapeel and backed away. A jolt of electricity zapped through the writhing black creature into the pale man's mouth.

The door to the throne room flew in with a BOOM, startling the slimy black serpent, which fell to the floor with a FLAP.

"Master," said another guard as he rushed in. "We've heard reports—"

"HOW DARE YOU INTERRUPT ME?" yelled the hooded figure. "I have almost broken him!"

"I'm so sorry, Master," the guard said, bowing, his voice shaking with fear. "Once I tell you the news, I'm sure you'll understand."

"Well, speak, you idiot, speak!" the hooded figure said. He picked up the zapeel and held it over the tank. It angrily flopped into the water with a SPLASH.

"Don't worry, my pretty," said the hooded figure, leaning in and tapping the glass lovingly. "You can feast on this fool if his story is not worthy of this interruption."

"A ship has crash-landed a mile from here, in the Gorgon Rift," the guard finally spit out.

"Has it now . . . ," said the hooded figure, turning to the man. "Looks like this new development has spared your pitiful life . . . for now." He moved his fiery glare back to the guard. "And *you* will live to disappoint me another day. Send the Andromedans to greet our newest guests."

The guard ran out as quickly as he could.

"Meanwhile," the hooded figure said, motioning to another guard, "the Director here is doing a better job of holding his tongue than I thought. He's going to need a few more sessions with the splurtsar and its delicious truth serum. Fetch Murray."

"Murray?" asked the guard, confused.

"The mummy! Now, be quick!"

As the guard ran out, he said, "Murray's just not a mummy's name . . ."

The pale, gaunt man snickered.

Earlier That Night . . .

The huge iron ship lurched—Frederick, the old green patchwork monster, was straining as he used the electricity that gave him life to power the engines. Slowly the ship lifted toward the hole in the ceiling of the massive cave.

The giant wooden steering wheel spun out of control, knocking me back. It looked like something you'd see on an old pirate ship.

"Come on, guys, help me steer," I yelled as I scrambled back to my feet. "If we can't get above ground, we're totally toast!"

Grigore the vampire and Gordon ran over, and we grabbed the wheel as hard as we could together.

"To. The. Right," I said through gritted teeth.

Grigore and Gordon grunted along with me as we slowly turned the wheel to the right. It shook so hard in our hands that my body was vibrating.

"My teeth hurt," yelled Gordon, his bulging muscles straining the sleeves of his Rio Vista Middle School Athletics T-shirt. "It's like I ate too much sugar on a freezing cold day."

CHATTER CHATTER CHATTER!

Shane and Roy, the Bigfoot, ran over to help us.

"We're not gonna make it," wheezed Ben, staring bug-eyed out the cracked window. He took a giant hit off his asthma inhaler. "The ship's gaining speed, and we're about to hit the ceiling."

The other monsters huddled together for safety, grabbing on to anything that looked like it wouldn't fall off the ancient rocket ship.

I pressed all my weight against the wheel. "As hard as you can, guys," I yelled. "PUUUUUUUSHHHHH!"

The zombies stared blankly as we struggled with the wheel.

SCRAAAAAAPE!

The nose of the rocket dragged along the craggy, rocky ceiling, making even more cracks in the window.

Everything vibrated and shook. It seemed unlikely that the rusty old rocket would hold together much longer. Then suddenly, the shaking stopped and the ship lunged forward, knocking us all to the floor. We were out of the cave!

Once we lifted above the earth, the sounds of the engine quieted to a level just below mind-numbing. Then we started to accelerate.

"Aw yeah!" yelled Shane. "We did it."

There were cheers throughout the bridge.

He lifted his hand off the wheel to give me a high five.

"Um, not a good time," I said.

"Oh right, we should probably keep our hands on the wheel," said Shane.

The ship really picked up speed when we hit the clouds. It felt like we were being pulled into the floor of the bridge, then—

BOOM!

—we hit turbulence and bounced off the wheel, sliding in all different directions.

"We've got to keep the rocket going straight," I yelled. "Otherwise, we're never going to make it."

I struggled to my feet for a moment, but was forced down onto all fours by the insane g-forces. I crawled over to the wheel on my belly. Roy struggled to stop himself, but the hairy monster couldn't keep from sliding farther away.

"My fur!" he yelled. "Too slippery!"

I had to roll to the side to make sure the Bigfoot

didn't crash into me as he slid across the floor.

"The ship's at the wrong angle! I think we're heading back down," I yelled as I tried to grab ahold of Roy. There was no way we could keep the ship on the right course without the burly Bigfoot to help us steer. Even Grigore wasn't that strong.

"I can't . . . ," the Bigfoot gasped again, his teeth rattling just like ours, ". . . get a grip."

The ship began to descend back to earth, and Roy slid even farther from the wheel.

"Oh man," moaned a green-looking Ben. "I'm going to hurl."

"We need to help Roy get up here!" I yelled, struggling along with a group of monsters to hang on to the wheel. "I can't believe we rushed onto the ship without the Nurses! We could really use their muscle."

"Wait," yelled Nabila, who was pressed flat against one of the rusty metal walls of the bridge. "I've got an idea!"

"What is it?" I asked. "Hurry!"

"Grigore!" Nabila yelled as we picked up speed, plummeting toward the earth. "Call the other vampires from the cargo hold with your mind. Bring them to us. Bring them to us as bats."

Grigore began to concentrate, his eyes wandering away in a daze. But his strength at the wheel held.

Soon, three vampire bats awkwardly flapped into

the room, their confused squeaks saying, *Wait, why are we here?*

"Nibble all the fur off Roy!" said Nabila.

"WHAT?!" yelled Roy. "No way!"

The bats squeaked in confusion, flapping hard to avoid the flying glass as different meters and gauges exploded.

"Just do it!" I yelled to the vampire bats.

"Nooooooo!" yelled Roy.

But the vampire bats swarmed Roy and did as I commanded.

BZZZZRRRRRPPPPP!

Their little fangs worked fast, as fast as the fastest electric razor. In a flash of fur, a very pink and very naked Roy appeared.

"Get over here! We need your monster strength," I yelled, and an embarrassed Roy crawled up the floor and grabbed the wheel.

"Arrrrrggghhhhhh," we grunted hard as we turned the wheel, and we could feel the ship rise into the air once again.

Once Roy had helped push the wheel down, he gave me an angry glare.

"You could have just had them take the fur off my paws, you know," he said.

"It wasn't *my* idea," I retorted. "Nabila?"

We looked over to the spot on the wall of the bridge

where she had been pressed, but she was gone. Looking down, we saw a pile of tangled brown hair, a fanny pack, and glasses.

"Better safe than sorry," she mumbled.

The ship blasted even faster into space, higher and higher, until . . .

"Why is it so quiet?"asked Ben, turning even greener. "My stomach feels like we're still climbing. Ugh."

"Look!" said Nabila, pointing out the window.

"We're in space!" I yelled. "We made it! The autopilot should take us from here—the crazy inventor said in his message that the rocket was already set on a course to the moon. The moooooooooooon!"

I relaxed my grip. Shane and the monsters shared worried looks as they all slowly let go of the wheel.

The ship kept moving along its trajectory.

There was a great cheer on the bridge.

"Chris, look!" Nabila said, pointing at my feet. "You're floating!"

"You too!" said Gordon, pointing at Nabila.

I pushed my feet down onto the floor, and shot up toward the ceiling. "Weeeee're innnnnn spaaaaaaaaaaace! Wahoo!"

The Monsters and Me in Zero-G

"Aw, man, this is AWESOME!" I yelled, corkscrewing through the air. "I can't believe it! We're going to the moon! THE MOON!"

Landing with an OOOF on one of the control panels, I looked up at all the doodads and whirligigs.

"I feel like I'm in a dream," I said.

"It looks more like a *nightmare*, with all of Gallow Manor's monsters on board," said Nabila. She'd spent the previous twenty minutes attempting to clean up the shattered bits of the ship and chewed-up Bigfoot fur that floated around the bridge.

Shane high-fived a passing zombie.

The zombie cartwheeled backward off the bridge.

"Stop messing around," said Nabila. "We've got to figure out what we're going to do when we get to the moon. We don't even know where Murrayhotep is taking Director Z. 'To him,' Murrayhotep kept saying."

"I know," I said. "And it freaks me out to think of who—or what—we're going to find on the moon. But we should have enough time before we get there to figure it all out—how to get Z and the pendant back. I know we should be worried, and I am, but this is by far the greatest moment of my life. So just give me a few minutes to take it all in."

Shane pushed off a wall, grabbed Nabila, and twirled her around in the middle of the room.

"Okay, fine!" she said, giggling. "But then let's get serious."

Ben's face was smashed against a glass porthole. He stared out at the blue planet that was slowly receding behind us.

"Wow," said Ben as the ship rocketed deeper into space. "Earth is so small."

"Dude, you realize you're upside down, right?" asked Gordon.

"Right-side up, upside down, it's all the same," Ben said.

"If we don't remember which way is which, I think something bad will happen," said Gordon, who had strapped himself into a chair next to a burned-out panel.

"I hope we didn't need any of these controls."

Behind me, I heard Pietro and Howie, two of the old werewolves, discussing how fun it was to transform in zero-g.

"This is great," said Howie with a crooked grin. "It's so much easier. Fast. Like . . . POOF! But how do you transform into a wolf without crashing against a wall?"

"Push yourself away from a wall just before you start to transform," replied Pietro. "Watch . . ."

Pietro kicked off the bridge of the spaceship with a "YEAHHHHOOOOOOWWWWWL" as he transformed.

"Wait for MEEEEEEHHHHOOOOOOWWWWL," Howie said, transforming with ease as he followed.

"Watch it, furballs!" someone screamed.

"Get out of your chair, Gordon," Nabila said, pushing off Gordon's face to fly toward me. "You're missing out."

"Whatever, Crazy Hair," Gordon said, pointing at Nabila's head, which, thanks to the zero-g, was a huge, floating, jet-black mess.

"Sorry," she said, "I didn't have a chance to pack a hat while we were rushing dozens of monsters onto this Victorian-era spacecraft."

"This is unbelievable," gasped Shane, who had joined Ben at the porthole.

"How far have we traveled?" asked Nabila.

"I really wish that I could make sense of these

controls," I replied. "It's unlike anything I've ever seen on *Star Wars* or *Star Trek*."

"*Star Blech* is more like it," said Gordon.

"Boy, zero-g makes you really cranky," said Shane.

"I just don't trust anywhere I can't play football," Gordon said.

"Just wait until we get to the moon," I said. "Even *I'll* be able to throw a fifty-yard pass there—just one-sixth the gravity of Earth! Oh man, it's going to be *great*!"

"Once we rescue Director Z from some form of evil that waits to crush us," said Ben. "Then you can have your football game."

A few of the old witches walked onto the bridge, dodging everyone and everything floating past them. "Everyone's safe down in the cargo hold," said Katherine, the oldest of them. "One of the zombies fell to pieces with all the shaking, but we took care of her before all the parts could float away."

"How are you walking!?!" asked Shane.

The three gray old ladies cackled, and Griselda walked in holding up a jar of gooey . . . something.

"What is that?" I asked. "I bet there's some essence of spiderweb and eye of newt in there . . ."

Gordon practically leaped out of his chair in excitement, but grabbed it quickly again to keep from floating away. "Hey, Griselda, bring some of that newt juice over here."

"Oh, it's not anything but marmalade," said Griselda.

"Why do you always think the marmalade is something gross?" Shane asked me.

I had no answer.

Griselda slathered a generous amount of marmalade onto Gordon's shoes, and he was able to stand on the floor once again.

"Anyone else?" asked Griselda.

"No, we're having too much fun," replied Nabila, who was spinning like a top while looking out the big window at all the stars.

"Suit yourself," said Gordon. "But you'll be sorry. Griselda, are my muscles less likely to shrink now that I'm walking? Chris, how long until we reach the moon and some gravity?"

I turned to one of the many gauges that slowly, creakily turned on the massive control panel, when I was struck in the face with a squeaking furry object.

"Aw, get off!" I yelled.

The bat bounced off my face, scratching me slightly with its rough wings, and corkscrewed wildly into . . .

"My hair!" Nabila screamed. "Ahhhhhh! Get out! Get out!"

She reached up to try to untangle the bat, but it just squeaked louder and got even more tangled.

"Judging by the squeaks, I think that's Grigore," said Ben as he kicked off Shane's rump to float over to Nabila.

"I don't care *who* it is!" she screeched. "Just get him out of my hair."

By the time Ben reached Nabila, Grigore's mad flapping was dragging her through the air in the opposite direction.

"Wait!" said Ben. "Stop flapping, Grigore!"

"I think he's panicking because he doesn't know how to fly in zero-g," said Shane. "But Ben will be able to untangle him as soon as he stops flapping and Nabila calms down."

"See," said Gordon. "This is why I'm sticking to the floor. Literally."

A helmet from one of the space suits floated past Gordon, and he snatched it up.

"Extra protection," Gordon said. "So how long is this going to take, Chris?"

"Hmmm," I said, trying to ignore Nabila's screams as Grigore dragged her off the bridge. "I'm not sure . . ."

I gazed up at the gauges that had survived the voyage, and scratched my head.

"We're going to get there in ten hours!" I said.

"Aw, that totally sucks!" yelled Gordon.

"What do you mean, 'totally sucks'?" I asked. "It took the first Apollo astronauts four days, bonehead. This is amazing! We might even have to slow down before we hit the moon. The moon! I might pass out from the excitement."

"Are you sure it's not the zero-g that's going to make you pass out?" asked Shane.

We stared at the moon as it grew larger in the window. "No, it's definitely the excitement," I said. "I just never thought I'd actually go to the moon. I mean, I had hoped and dreamed. But this is amazing! It's unbelievable. It's like I've been training for this moment for my entire life. I just always thought it would be with NASA—"

"I hope this tin can we're flying in protects us from solar flares and cosmic rays," added Shane.

I shivered at the thought of cosmic rays blasting through my body.

"I've got to admit," said Gordon, "I always thought you were pretty dorky for staring at the moon all the time. But all that dorkiness really paid off. Because I have absolutely no idea what cosmic rays are."

The sound of retching floated up the stairs into the bridge.

"Aw, man," Ben moaned as he spun into the room. "This is worse than the Barfitron."

"He got sick chasing Grigore and me around the ship," Nabila said, floating in behind him.

"Plus," Ben said, "I inhaled some of Roy's hair, which is floating all over the ship."

"I did the best I could," said Nabila. "There was more hair than I could handle!"

"Just burp a little," said Shane. "That always makes you feel better."

"That's a good idea," said Nabila, floating over to help him.

"WAIT," I yelled. "There's no such thing as burping in space!"

But it was too late.

Brace Yourselves
. . . for Vurp!

Ben tried to burp, but ended up blowing a pretty good collection of multicolored chunks all over the bridge.

"There's no gravity to push food down and air up in your stomach," I said, swatting a few chunks away. "The astronauts call it a 'wet burp.' I call it a 'vurp.'"

Just the sound of the word made Ben gag again. He closed his mouth tight, and two jets of wet vurp shot out his nose, spinning him backward a bit.

"Ugh, keep it in, dearie!" screeched Griselda, who was slathering a second coating of marmalade on Gordon's shoes.

"Sorrggggbbbllllllrrcchhh," said Ben, and let it loose

all over a zombie who had floated onto the bridge at the worst possible moment.

"Get it off me!" the zombie yelled. "Oh, it's terrible. Now I know what a sussuroblat feels like."

He shimmied and shook it off his rotting body.

"I've never seen a zombie move so fast," said Shane. "And I know some fast zombies."

The zombie's arm flew off and directly into the open mouth of Pietro in werewolf form.

GLLUUURP!

"That will make a tasty snack," said Shane.

But the arm was shaking so violently that it gagged Pietro.

He WHARFED up the arm along with a hairy wet mess.

"Oh man, a werehairball!" said Gordon. "Those are the worst. Pietro, I thought I told you to stop licking yourself so much!"

The mass danced around, started to growl and shake, and then got pulled apart by the lack of gravity.

"Bet everyone wishes they had a helmet on, huh?" taunted Gordon.

The bridge was now filled with a disgusting cloud of Ben's dinner, Roy's hair, and Pietro's hairball.

"Wait, why was the hairball growling so loudly?" asked Shane.

I peered out the window in shock.

"The moon!" I yelled. "It's so much closer than it should be! We're going insanely fast. Like, a hundred thousand miles per hour!"

"ARGGGHHH!" a scream came over the intercom, and the lights flickered.

I floated through the cloud of barf-hair and slammed my fist down on the intercom.

"We're coming in too fast!" I yelled. "You've got to reduce your energy, Frederick."

Bells began ringing through the ship, clanging like a large alarm clock.

The ship shook violently, and Nabila crashed onto a control panel, crazy hair first.

"OOOOOOF," she yelled as her head crunched down on a button.

"Nabila!" yelled Ben, swiping away the barf that was orbiting around his head. "I'm coming."

But Ben wasn't going anywhere—he couldn't get any footing.

Gordon kicked Ben in his butt, and Ben finally went flying over to Nabila.

"Oh, I'm okay," she said weakly as he crashed into her. "I think I inhaled your barf. I'm officially grossed out."

Ben grabbed Nabila and kicked off the control panel, just as another violent shudder caused it to spark and catch fire. The zombie floated over and began slapping the control panel with the arm he had lost, to put out the flames.

Frederick's "ARRGGGHHHHH" was even louder now.

"Frederick!" I yelled over the screech of the ship. "I know you're in pain, but you have to turn off your power completely, or we're going to come into the moon's orbit too fast and crash-land. But you need to give me one last burst of power when I tell you to. Can you do it?"

"YARRRGGGHHHHHH!" he yelled back.

"I'll take that as a 'yes,'" I said. "Wait until I say NOW!"

I turned to the monsters at the wheel. Roy had used his entire body to bear down on it, and I was suddenly glad that Nabila had had the vampire bats take off all his hair.

"Keep it steady!" I said. "When Frederick gives us the burst, you've got to turn it clockwise!"

"We're at five thousand feet and plummeting," yelled Shane from the altimeter.

"GET READY TO PULL THE NOSE UP!" I yelled.

"Four thousand . . ."

"Three thousand . . ."

"NOW, FREDERICK," I yelled.

The ship careened to the right, pushing every floating friend and monster into the back left of the bridge. Roy was able to hold on tight by sticking his pasty-pink arm under the spoke of the wheel when it turned back to the left.

"Arrrrrgh!" he screamed.

"ARRGGGHHHH," Frederick screamed over the intercom.

Shane was still clutching the altimeter and shot off the changing altitude as quick as a machine gun.

"Five hundred . . . four hundred . . . three hundred . . . two hundred . . ."

"HOLD ON!" I screamed.

"Hold on to what!?" Gordon yelled as his marmalade failed and he dropped onto the pile of monsters in the corner.

SCREEEEEEEBOOM!

Houston, the Eagle
Has Belly Flopped

"Hwaaaa!" I gasped for air, convinced the hull of the ship was wide open.

I could breathe... but pitch-black silence surrounded me. And because I could breathe, I could smell the mix of barf and wet monster hair. I was actually pretty glad I couldn't see it.

"Frederick?" I yelled. "FREDERICK!?"

No response.

"Guys?" I asked.

Soft moans floated up from the room. I couldn't tell where they were coming from. I couldn't even tell if we had landed right-side up.

"I don't even know where *I* am," I said.

"BUUUUUURP." Ben burped and sounded greatly relieved. "Well, I'm not vurping, so we must be on the moon. Did we land on the dark side?"

"That would be impossible. I think we crashed deep into the lunar surface and got buried in moon rock," I said.

"It's getting hotter by the second," said Nabila.

"This gravity feels so weird," Gordon said. "But at least we're not floating around uncontrollably anymore."

"Lights would help, though," said Shane. "Did we lose Frederick? What happened to the electricity?"

"I'm so glad all of you made it," I said. "I wouldn't have forgiven myself if you had died."

"No, I wouldn't have let you forgive yourself," Shane said. "Because I would have haunted you for all eternity."

"Like Quincy?" I asked.

"No, I'd be a cooler ghost than that little stinker," said Shane. "For one thing, I'd be older and wiser for all eternity."

"Yeah, by a whopping two years!" screeched Nabila. "Can we get on with it? We have to do something. I'm burning! What on earth are we doing?!"

"You mean, 'what on moon' are we doing," replied Ben.

"You know what I mean," she said. "Don't try being smarter than me, it's just never gonna happen."

"She's right," I said.

"Hey!" said Ben in protest.

"No, she's right that we need to move fast," I said. "Without the power cells to run the climate system, we'll get pretty toasty in this old tin."

"Why?" asked Gordon.

"During the lunar day, it can get as hot as two hundred fifty degrees," replied Shane.

"Oh right . . . ," said Gordon. "Yeah, of course, why didn't I think of that?"

"But not even that will last long," I said, "with sunset coming soon."

"Sunset?" asked Ben. "Now I'm confused. You said we weren't on the dark side of the moon."

"The dark side of the moon is only dark when looking from Earth," I said. "In actuality, every part of the moon gets two weeks of sunshine and two weeks of darkness."

"So, we're about to experience two weeks of darkness?" asked Shane.

"Yep," I said. "Well, darkness along with earth- and starshine."

"Uh-oh!" said Shane.

"Then we'll have to deal with the cold," I said. "So either way, we need to figure out the climate system."

From outside the ship, thunder rumbled.

"It vas a dark and stormy night . . . ," Grigore said, giggling.

"That's not possible," I said. "There's no weather on the moon."

"Then it must have been something else," Gordon said.

"But what?" Nabila asked.

BOOOOM. Again the sound of thunder.

"Now it's even closer," said Ben.

"Do you think they know we're here?" asked Shane.

"Who are 'they'?" Gordon asked.

"Guys, I'm frying!" yelled Nabila. "We've got to do something!"

"All right," I said. "I've got an idea, but I need to feel my way down to Frederick."

"I could use my night vision to guide you," said Grigore, and a clammy, dead hand wrapped itself around mine.

"On a dark and stormy night on the moon, the old vampire grabbed me in the dark," I said, and now I was the one who was giggling.

Grigore, despite his amazing vampire abilities, was still a goofy old man, and he just couldn't handle the low gravity. It had taken us far too long to get down into the darkness to speak with Frederick. It was getting really, really hot in the ship.

"I'm *melting*," Frederick moaned from his electric chair.

"Don't worry, buddy," I said. "I don't think you'll melt until at least eight hundred degrees."

"Okay, but I'm *thirsty*," he said.

"That, I can help you with," I said. "Grigore, go get some water from the supply closet."

"And get the werewolves," said Frederick.

"Werewolves?" I asked.

"I need a charge," he said.

"Oh of course!" I said, understanding what needed to happen.

While we waited in the hot darkness, Frederick gave me a status update. Since he had been plugged into the ship, he was the eyes of the ship as well as its energy supply.

"Oxygen levels dropping," he wheezed while I rubbed his back to comfort him. "My power near zero. Climate-control system overloaded. Find the control panel on the bridge, this big." He used his hands, which sparked slightly with electric charge, to show me how big. "Hit it and pull the short lever to turn it back on. I can't turn on the lights to help you find it. May be too much of a power drain, even with the werewolves' static charge. I'm so sorry."

"You did a great job," I said. "We made it! I'll figure out the climate control. You just charge up."

In the dark, I could hear the werewolves pad into the room. I moved away from Frederick and heard the sound of their dry old fur rubbing up against Frederick's legs and the legs of the electric chair he used to connect with the ship. After a while, there was a soft glow coming off of Frederick, and I could see the werewolves rushing around in a circle, their tongues almost dragging on the floor. Their eyes bugged.

Frederick leaned back with a sigh, taking in their static charge.

"Take breaks, guys," I said. "Or you'll pass out."

The werewolves stopped every once in a while and nuzzled his leg, a great spark flying from their wet noses into him.

CRACK!

"Ah!" yelled Frederick. "Stop it!"

CRACK!

"That tickles!"

CRACK!

"I mean it! Stop it!"

The werewolves laughed a growly laugh.

"Play nice," I said. "He's had a rough ride. Grigore, give Frederick his water and then help me down to the cargo hold. I have an idea."

Down in the cargo hold, the monsters were buzzing with anticipation.

"Did we make it?" one asked in the dark.

"Are you dead, now, too?" asked another.

"Yes and no. But I can't answer any more questions until later," I said impatiently.

Once I heard from Frederick that his batteries were too low to power the lights, I knew what I had to do.

"All the zombies, gather around," I said.

I heard shuffling and heavy breathing, and was suddenly surrounded by the six zombies of Gallow Manor Retirement Home. I could tell because of the outrageously rotten smell, a stink made even worse by the heat.

"Okay, guys, maybe just back off a little," I said. "I'm still breathing, you know?"

There were a few moans, and then the zombies obeyed, backing away and making the room smell "somewhat funky" as opposed to "insanely barf-inducing."

"Sorry, Boss," said one of the zombies. "We ran out of the breath mints you gave us pretty early in the trip."

"It's okay," I said. "I need you guys to use the air lock at the back to exit the spaceship, then walk up to the front of the ship and clear away all the moon rocks that are covering the bridge's viewport."

"You got it, Boss," they said. "Just tell us what to do."

"Feel your way to the back of the cargo hold and pull the lever," I said.

There was some shuffling as the zombies searched for the lever, and then a loud clank. With a metallic SCREECH, the door rolled open.

I could hear them shuffle into the air lock, so I walked over with Grigore to close the door behind them.

"Wait until we close this door before you open the second one," I said to the zombies.

Grigore waited with a hand on the lever. "Use your strength," I said to him, and with a grunt, he clanked the door shut.

I pressed an ear against the door and could hear the zombies open the second door.

Air WHOOOSHED out of the air lock, and then there was silence.

The utter silence of zombies in space.

"We're cooked if they can't find their way," I said to Grigore. "Let's go back to the bridge and wait."

If the Moon Were Made of Cheese, It Would Melt

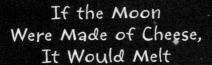

"So, what's the deal?" said Shane. "I hear a lot of the monsters calling you 'Boss' these days. Even I can't get the zombies to do much, no matter how many brains I bribe them with."

"I'm only telling you because I trust you," I said, grabbing his sweaty shoulders and pulling him toward me. "You can't tell the others, and you can never let the info loose, not even under torture."

"Okay, okay!" he said. "What is it?"

"I'm holding a pendant," I whispered directly into Shane's sweaty ear. "I'm an astronaut . . . and a Director."

"What?!" Shane yelled.

"I'll explain later," I said. "But we just have to hope

this works first. You're sweating. And you never sweat."

"Is Frederick dead?" asked Nabila. I jumped in the dark, wondering if she had heard my secret.

"No, but he tells me that he only has enough power for the climate system. We just don't have enough light to see what we're doing and fix it."

"Why can't he turn on the lights?" asked Shane.

"Because that would use up what little power he had, which we need—"

"—for the climate system, got it!" Shane said, finishing my sentence. "Whew, it's hot in here."

"What's the plan?" asked Ben.

"I'm hoping that before the sun sets on our part of the moon, the zombies can remove all the moon rocks that are covering the viewport. Then we'll use the light to fix the climate system with Frederick's instructions."

"Aren't the zombies gonna get cooked?" asked Gordon.

"I don't think so," I replied. "I'm more worried about them wandering off looking for moon brains."

"And if they do get cooked or wander off?" asked Shane.

"Then we'll most likely freeze in the hull of this ship, when the sun sets," I said.

"Goooooo, zombies!" he yelled.

We waited and waited and waited, frying like little chicken drumsticks, until . . .

"Wait, what is that sound?" croaked Pietro between pants. Circling Frederick had made his throat dry.

"I don't hear anything," I said.

"Scraping . . . ," said Pietro.

I listened hard and heard it!

With a big scrape, part of the viewport was exposed. A zombie with a very big grin peered in and gave me a thumbs-up.

The rays of sun took Grigore by surprise. He threw up his hand to cover his eyes, but the rest of him began to smoke terribly.

"Arrrgh," he wailed. "I'm just not as old as I used to be!"

"Gordon," I said, "drag Grigore out of those rays. Grigore, you've got to go down to the cargo hold. The sun is extremely strong on the moon—there's no atmosphere to shield it!"

Soon the rest of the viewport was exposed, and I took a quick few seconds to look out at the moonscape.

"Wow . . . ," I said. "I can't believe it."

I was so excited, I drooled a little.

"Believe it!" yelled Nabila. "Look at the sun!"

She pointed at the sun as it sank quickly behind one of the moon's many peaks.

"We don't have much time," I said, jumping back into the room and stumbling across the shards of metal, barf, and hair that covered the floor. The witches, who had all been napping, suddenly woke up.

"Are we there yet?" one of them cackled.

The glow of the sun was already starting to fade as I scrambled frantically to look for the control panel that Frederick had described.

"We need to find a panel the size of Herr Direktor Detlef's fish tank," I said. "But I just don't remember seeing anything like that in here."

Ben pointed to the wall above one of the control panels and said, "It's over here! I remember barfing on it."

I ran over the metallic debris in the middle of the bridge, trying not to trip over the larger chunks or slip on the wet barf and werewolf hair.

"How do we get it open?" Shane asked.

I slammed my fist against the far right side, and it swung open.

My eyes crossed as I looked deep into the massive control panel. It was huge mess of levers, metal pipes, wires, glass tubes, and strange dials. You'd need to have an engineering degree from the 1800s to make sense of any of it.

"Uhhhhh . . . ," I said to nobody. "Frederick said to look for the shortest lever, but these all look exactly the same size!"

"What happens if you pull the wrong one?" Nabila asked.

"I have no idea," I said. "But I'm assuming it would be terrible."

The rays of sun that had been pointed at the panel disappeared.

I looked up to the window and saw that there was more dirt and rock that could be cleared away.

"Shane, keep the zombies there!" I said. "Get them to clear out that last bit of debris!"

Shane waved madly at the zombies. They wandered back to the window, and he started to pantomime what he wanted them to do.

"MOVE. THE. ROCK," he said. "MOVE. THE. DIRT."

"They can't hear you," I said, peering once again into the ancient control panel.

"It helps me figure out how to move my body," said Shane. "DOOOOO. IT."

Soon, a little more light shone into the control panel, and in the very back, past a tangle of wires and pipes, I could see . . .

"The short lever!" I yelled, and reached in to pull it down.

The hiss of air conditioning sounded through the bridge.

"Oh, it's sooooo good," said Nabila, and she rushed over to a barfy pile of scrap metal, pushed it aside, and shoved her face in the vent that was there.

All over the ship, monsters and kids alike sighed a collective "ahhhhhhhh . . ."

A loud banging sounded throughout the bridge.

BOOM BOOM BOOM.

A few of the zombies stood at the window, pounding furiously.

"They're freaking out," said Ben. "Why are they freaking out?"

Soon, all the zombies were going crazy. They pushed up frantically against the window.

"What are they trying to yell at us?" asked Nabila.

Some had their backs squished against the glass, looking out toward the dark.

"Is something out there with them?" asked Ben. "Oh, please tell me there's nothing out there with them."

Three huge figures rose above the six zombies— they looked like massive, swollen heads, throbbing with green goo, mouths filled with razor-sharp teeth. Tentacles floated below the heads, swaying softly in front of the zombies.

"Oh man, there *is* something out there with them," yelled Ben.

"RUN!" yelled Nabila.

But the zombies were too terrified to notice, even if they could have heard her.

Vurp Invaders

The zombies stood frozen in front of the bizarre, disgusting aliens, who gnashed their teeth and reached out their tentacles to probe their prey.

"Gah, they're disgusting!" yelled Gordon. "Like the worst zit times a hundred. Is that green stuff in their heads pus? Ugh!"

"I was really hoping I wouldn't run into an alien on this trip," said Ben.

"I figured aliens would show up," said Nabila. "I mean, we've pulled a whole bunch of old monsters into space. It was bound to happen."

The aliens began oozing fluorescent green and yellow from their mouths, forming a cloud around the zombies. Five of the zombies ran, but one was left in shock, staring.

The creatures' big bulbous heads began to palpitate and squirm. Somehow, I swore that I heard burping.

The trapped zombie turned away from the creatures and looked at us through the glass. There was literally nothing we could do.

"Help me!" he screamed.

"How can we hear that?" I asked.

And suddenly, BOOM, another great peel of thunder sounded on the ship, just like the ones from before.

Waves of sound rippled through the zombie, liquefying him and spraying a blast of blood and guts all over the window. He looked like a fly that made the mistake of buzzing in front of a Mack truck.

Soon we could hear a slurping noise, and all the zombie's parts were lifted off the viewport and into the waiting mouths of the creatures.

Satisfied with their meal, they pressed up against the glass, feeling the window with their tentacles.

Howie the werewolf transformed and ran right up to the viewport, snapping his dog teeth and scraping at the window with his paw.

"What are you doing?" I said. "You probably shouldn't let them know that we're in here!"

"GRRRRRRRRR BARK BARK BARK."

"They're starting to notice us," warned Shane.

The heads closed in and started exhaling the green goo once again. It hung in front of the ship, and for sure this time I could hear a gentle BURP BURP BURP sound. Suddenly, their tentacles suctioned up against the glass and pulled.

"HOW IS THAT POSSIBLE!?!?" I screamed. "They shouldn't be able to do that."

"What do you mean?" asked Gordon.

"The moon exists in the vacuum of space," replied Nabila. "And in a vacuum, the suction required to grab the glass just isn't possible."

"I think they're vurping a cloud around them that is capable of transmitting sound in space," said Shane.

"Space Vurp?" I asked.

The strange aliens leaned back hard, and the crack in the glass that had started at takeoff got a little bit bigger.

"BARK BARK BARK BARK BARK."

"Stop it, Howie!" I commanded. And Howie HOWWWWWWWLED.

The ship shook, and the aliens backed away from the glass as more moon rocks and moondust poured over the viewport. Somewhere, someone laughed a deep, gut-trembling laugh. The laughter shook the ship even further and we were tumbled onto our butts. Shards of barfy metal tore into our jeans.

"OW!"

The bridge was dark and silent again.

"Sorry if I did that," wheezed Howie. "I was just really upset."

"No, I think you did good," said Shane. "I'm just not sure you did it alone."

"What do you mean?" asked Gordon.

"I have a theory—" said Shane.

"Now I'm freezing," said Nabila, cutting him off.

"Oh, just please, please, please tell me we didn't break the climate system," I said.

There was a soft whirring sound, and the climate system and lights came up again. There was a loud pop of static from the intercom.

"Chris." The staticky voice of Frederick came over the intercom. "Oxygen levels normal."

There was more static, and then . . .

"You really need to come down to the cargo hold," Griselda's voice cut in. "You are not going to believe this."

I could hear the excited grunts of monsters.

We entered the cargo hold to see the monsters gathered around a massive tear that had opened up in the metal floor. A thin canyon made of moon rock could be seen below it.

"What in the world?" I asked.

Nabila replied in her usual way. "You mean, 'what in the moon?'"

"You know what I mean," I said.

"After Howie howled," said Griselda, "this crack opened up in the floor."

"I guess that's what shook us up so badly," I said.

"The air is slightly smelly," said Medusa, who leaned down near the crack.

A snake from her head slithered into the crack.

"But it's totally breathable," hissed the snake.

"Thanks, Bruce," said Shane.

"That must be where the oxygen is coming from," I said. "Incredible."

Shane walked over to the crack and got on his hands and knees, trying to poke his head into it.

"Be careful it doesn't close back up!" said Gordon.

"The crack is too thin for me to see anything. Can you see anything else?" Shane asked the snake.

"No," hissed Bruce. "But there is a light coming from down there . . . somewhere."

"I think we've got to explore this," said Shane. "We know what's up on the surface of the moon, and it's not good."

"But how can we, if it's too thin to crawl into?" I asked.

"Maybe we chisel away at the rock and try to make

it wider?" suggested Gordon.

"Give it a try," Nabila said to Roy.

Roy walked over to the crack and lifted his naked arm.

WHACK!

The ship shook again, but nothing happened.

"Ow," said Roy, and he cradled his hurt hand. "I miss my fur."

"Oh dearie," said Katherine. "I might have packed something that can help you. Come over here with me."

"Maybe we shouldn't try to widen it until we figure out where it goes," said Nabila.

"How can we figure that out?" I asked.

"Let's send out some scouts," Nabila responded.

"Scouts?" asked Gordon.

"A fleet of vampire bats," said Nabila.

There were three loud pops behind us. Grigore, Vlad, and Camilla, in the form of vampire bats, fluttered in front of Nabila.

"Vhat do you vant us to do?" they asked.

"See where the crack leads. Observe and report back to us. If you see anyone or anything, don't let them see or hear you. Got it?"

"Got it!" they squeaked, and swooped quickly into the crack.

"Now we wait," I said.

"Guys, I think I know why the crack opened in the

first place," said Shane.

"What's your big theory?" asked Gordon.

"The moon opened up the crack," said Shane confidently.

"What!?!" the entire cargo hold of monsters and kids said in unison.

"Wait, hear me out," said Shane.

"Go on," I said.

"Remember, back on Earth, the huge map of the moon in the space room where we found the phonograph record that led us to the ship?"

"YES!" the entire room responded.

"I don't think it was a map of a moon that looked like it had a real face," said Shane. "I think it was a picture!"

"A picture of the real man in the moon?" I asked. "But he doesn't really exist. There's not a man in the moon, just like it's not really made of cheese."

"Or is it . . . ," asked Gordon, staring at the rock.

"Did you see Roy just hit that moon rock?" asked Nabila. "I think it's safe to say the moon isn't cheese."

"Agreed," said Shane. "I knew just from the landing that the moon wasn't made of cheese. It's too hard. But that's not the point."

"What is the point, Shane?" I asked, flabbergasted.

"The point is, Howie howled, and the moon responded," Shane said. "Howie, what were you feeling when you howled?"

"I was howling for protection," responded Howie. "I was howling for help."

"And we got both," Shane said. "Those nasty creatures aren't bothering us anymore, and we might have had the next path in our quest to save Director Z open up right in front of us."

There was a scraping, flapping noise, and the vampire bats flew out of the crack under the cargo hold. Covered in moondust, one by one they transformed back into vampires with loud POPs.

"Ve must hurry," said Grigore, rushing over to me. "Ve have seen Murray and Director Z, and Murray is going to kill him!"

Finding Z

The monsters freaked out.

"Director Z!" A werewolf howled. "No!"

"That murderer!" screamed a banshee.

A few of the monsters started clawing at the crack, desperate to make it wider.

"Wait," I said. "Slow down. What's happening? You saw Murray and Director Z?"

"Yes," said Grigore. "The crack leads to a system of caves. If you follow the glowing globes down far enough, you'll find a prison. Ve saw Murray . . ."

"Murray the mummy?" asked Shane. "You mean Murrayhotep?"

"Yes, our Murray," responded Grigore. "Ve saw

Murray drag Director Z out of his dirty underground cell into a room with a disgusting creature that burps out a tarry ooze."

"I think he called it a 'splurtsar,'" interrupted Vlad with a shudder.

"Yes, that vas it," said Grigore. "I think the ooze is meant to control Director Z's mind and make him give up all our secrets! A disgusting truth serum! The vile creature burps it up directly into the mouth of Director Z."

"So he's not trying to kill Director Z?" I asked.

"I don't know!" said Grigore. "I think so. Murray said, 'I don't care vhat Master says. I'm going to kill you and say it vas an accident. He'll thank me later.' But he might have been just trying to scare Director Z."

"Either way," I said, "we need to get down there as quickly as possible."

"It von't be easy to get down there," said Grigore. "Ve vere lucky ve made it. There vas a strong laser barrier that ve had to fly through. I singed my fur!"

Grigore turned around, and there was a burn mark up the back of his head.

"Let me help you with that," said Shane. He licked his fingertips and put out the pieces of hair that were still smoldering.

"But we've got to try," I said. "You heard what Murrayhotep said! What if he actually means it?"

"What do we do?" asked Ben.

"The first thing we need to do is figure out how to widen this crack," said Nabila.

"The werewolves should howl," said Shane. "They should howl asking the moon for help. They should howl asking the moon to open up this crack so we can actually fit into it."

"All right, then, do it!" I commanded the werewolves.

"HOOOOOOWWWWWWWL!"

The room shook. With a blast of moondust, the narrow entrance in the floor of the cargo hold opened up into the moon caves below.

I rushed up to the newly widened crack and could see that there were craggy moon rocks jutting out along the way to the first glowing globe that Grigore had mentioned.

"We should be able to climb down now," I said.

"So, what's the plan?" asked Shane.

"We shouldn't bring everyone down there," I replied. "Just a few. The humans, the vampires, and the werewolves. Otherwise, Murrayhotep will hear us coming from a mile away."

"Well, let's get going then!" yelled Nabila. "We don't know how much time we actually have."

She jumped into the crack and started navigating her way deeper inside.

"All right," I said. "Let's do this. Vampire bats in the lead . . ."

With a POP, the vampires turned back into bats.

". . . werewolves take up the guard in the back. Nabila, slow down!"

We all made our way into the crack. I looked up to see the werewolves pad down after us, and the faces of concerned monsters surrounding the entryway.

"Somebody go see if Frederick needs anything!" I yelled, and added, "And the zombies are probably scared to death in the air lock. Let them in—I almost forgot them."

We reached the first glowing globe, which was connected directly to the moon rock with a crude plug. It swayed slightly in the gravity of the moon.

"I wonder what that is," said Shane.

"I have no idea," I said, putting my hands in front of the glowing globe. "It's not hot."

One of the werewolves nipped at Shane's pant leg.

"All right, we're going, we're going!" insisted Shane.

We followed the vampire bats deeper down into the moon.

"The deeper we go, the warmer it gets," said Nabila.

"And the stinkier," Ben added.

"And the stickier," I said.

"Maybe the moon is made of cheese after all," said Shane.

We all listened to our sneakers SCHLOOP, SCHLIP, SCHLOPP as we walked deeper, passing globe after globe.

Suddenly, the greenish glow on the moon rock turned to red as we rounded a corner, revealing a tunnel crisscrossed with lasers.

"A security barrier!" I said. "That's what singed your fur?"

One of the bats fluttered down to me. I could see the small burn mark on its head.

"Yes!" it squeaked.

A loud scream echoed through the tunnel from the other side of the barrier.

"Sounds like we found Director Z," said Shane.

"We've got to hurry!" I said. "Werewolves, can you try howling again? Ask the moon for help!"

The werewolves raised their heads and opened their muzzles. Immediately, the vampire bats flew down into their necks, choking them.

"What are you doing?" I asked.

"If we can hear Director Z's scream," said Nabila, "whoever's with Director Z will hear them howl."

"Of course," I said. "Sorry, guys."

"Now what?" Gordon asked.

With a squeak, Grigore floated over to a small

numeric pad set into the wall of moon rock, ten feet or so in front of the laser beams.

Ben rushed over to have a look.

"This must turn it on and off," he said.

He leaned in closer to the pad.

"Three numbers are crusted in moondust," he said. "Three, five, and seven. Those must be the three numbers you type in to turn it off!"

"Well, give it a try," I said.

Ben typed in 3-7-5.

With a soft electrical hum, the lasers moved a few feet down the tunnel toward us.

"There are five other combinations of the three numbers," said Ben. "I'm going to try again."

Ben typed in 7-3-5.

A soft electrical hum.

The lasers moved down the tunnel again. Now they were only six feet in front of us. The werewolves backed down in fear.

Ben typed in 7-5-3.

A soft electrical hum.

Four feet away.

Ben typed in 5-3-7.

A soft electrical hum.

Two feet away.

Everyone moved back. Everyone but Ben.

"Only two more possible combinations," said Ben.

He put his finger up to the three.

"Be careful, Ben!" screeched Nabila.

3-5-7

We could hear the hum of the lasers as they moved past the keypad.

Ben jumped back and, with a SQUISH, landed on the floor of gooey moon rock.

Nabila ran over to help him up.

"Maybe we should let the werewolves howl after all," I said. "It might be our only chance."

"Wait!" Ben said. "There's only one combination left, and I can reach my hand through the laser beams."

He rushed back over to the keypad.

"What if you're wrong?" Nabila yelled. "What if there's another number?"

"Then I'm toast," he said. "But I'm sure of it."

He slowly moved his arm in between two of the beams and reached up to the keypad. Nabila rushed toward him, but he held up his other hand.

"Stop," he said. "If I'm wrong, we don't both have to die."

She stopped.

The werewolves whimpered.

Ben looked at me and winked.

Ben typed in 5-7-3.

A soft electrical hum . . .

. . . and with a soft *click*, the lasers turned off.

"Yeah," I said, and ran up to give Ben a hug. "I'm so glad you were right."

The others dog piled us in joy . . .

. . . when another scream from Director Z pierced the air.

"Let's go!" said Ben.

Saving Z

We ran down the tunnel, and with every step, Director Z's screams got louder.

"Is this the way?" I asked Grigore as we came up against a wall with a small passageway crudely drilled down the center.

He fluttered down and turned into a human again.

"I'm sorry, Boss," said Grigore. "I forgot about this part. I vas so worried about Director Z."

I scrambled up into the passageway, but was barely able to wiggle my shoulders in, even if I crawled. It was insanely hot and sticky inside.

"Not even the werewolves are going to be able to fit into that," I said, pulling my head out of the hole.

Another scream came through the passageway.

"How far is Z?" I asked Grigore.

"He's just through this passagevay and around the corner," said Grigore.

"What if we covered ourselves with this moon juice?" said Shane, swiping at the ground.

The werewolves didn't wait. They started rolling around on the ground, their fur squishing into it with a SQUELCH SQUIRCH SQUALTCH. They jumped up and squeezed into the passageway one by one. When the last paws disappeared, I looked over at Shane.

"Great idea," I said, and reached down to grab some moon muck. I slathered it on my arms.

"We don't have time!" said Shane, and he dropped to the ground and started to roll around just like the werewolves had.

We all followed his lead.

I looked over to see Ben's face even whiter than usual, covered with the liquid moon.

"Let's hurry up before it dries," said Shane.

The bats flew into the passageway, and Shane jumped up to follow.

All my friends were able to squeeze through, and it was finally my turn.

I put my shoulders in again, and this time they slipped through. I crawled and clawed through the darkness, barely able to breathe because of how tight it was.

I stopped to take a break, overwhelmed by the intense heat in the passageway.

"How much farther?" I hissed, starting to panic.

But before anyone could answer, Nabila, who was ahead of me, POPPED through the other side, and the strange glow of another globe came through the passageway.

I went to move again, but was stuck.

"Nooo," I said, and dug my nails into the moon rock, sliming forward like a deranged, trapped snail.

Shane grabbed my hand and pulled me through with a wet . . .

POP!

I tumbled to the ground, and Ben put his finger up to his lips. "*Shhhhh.*"

"Do do do it it it," Director Z's voice echoed from around the corner. "Go ahead. Feed me to the splurtsar."

"I wonder what this splurtsar's going to look like?" Gordon asked.

"Something tells me we're about to find out," replied Shane.

"*Feed* you to the splurtsar?" chuckled Murray. "I will feed his black nectar *to you* until you choke."

"Gwarrbbllebll," Director Z said. It sounded like he was already choking.

"Wow, Murrayhotep sounds young," said Gordon. "Really young."

"And angry," Ben added.

"Well, that's nothing new," said Shane.

"Shhhh," Nabila whispered. "Lower your voices. We don't want Murrayhotep to hear us."

"Everyone get close," I said. Everyone leaned in, and the bats flitted quietly overhead.

"Whatever this splurtsar is, maybe we can use it to our advantage. Bats, I want you to fly in to distract Murrayhotep. Once his attention is on you, squeak really loud. Pietro and Howie, when you hear the squeaking, rush in and tackle Murrayhotep. Don't hurt him, just pin him down and chew on his neck a little. We need to ask him who he's working for, and why he betrayed us. We'll pull the splurtsar off Director Z."

I looked at everyone and asked, "Ready?"

Everyone nodded.

"All right," I whispered. "Let's do it."

The bats flitted away.

For a few moments, we couldn't hear anything but Director Z's drinking and choking.

BLURGH. BLACHOUGH. BLUURGH.

"Hey!" yelled Murrayhotep. "Get out of my face, you flying rats!"

I couldn't hear any squeaking, but I was pretty sure Murrayhotep was distracted. I slapped the werewolves on their haunches, and they took off around the corner.

Murrayhotep was halfway through calling for a

guard when his yell was cut off by the werewolves. "GUA—OOF!"

"Good boys!" I yelled, and ran around the corner along with my friends.

Murrayhotep struggled with the werewolves on one side of a small cave. On the other side of the cave, a rotten little creature with red eyes stared at us as it filled a bug-eyed Director Z with black goo. It was the size of a pig, but with the trunk of an elephant. The trunk wrapped around Director Z's neck and into his mouth.

GLURP. BLURP. BLORP.

"The splurtsar!" I yelled.

"You?" yelled Murrayhotep. "Not *you*!"

"Wow, you are lookin' good, Murrayhotep!" said Shane. "Doesn't he look fitter? Not so dusty?"

Murrayhotep struggled under the werewolves. They tightened their toothy grips, but I knew they wouldn't harm him. I'd given them very specific orders.

But Murray didn't know that, and he held still.

The splurtsar tightened its grip on Director Z, dug in its stubby feet, and suctioned onto Director Z's mouth and nose.

We rushed over to Director Z, who flailed under the uninterrupted flow of black nectar. I yanked at the trunk, but it was sealed into place with a mucousy suction cup.

"Ugh, Gordon," I said, pulling at the trunk. "Grab the splurtsar! Hurry!"

The splurtsar let out an annoyed SQUUUUUUEEEE through its trunk when Gordon grabbed it, spraying black nectar all over my face. It snapped its little teeth in anger.

"I vouldn't get that in your mouth!" yelled Grigore, now back in human form. "Don't even sniff it in! Remember, it's a truth serum."

"Ugh," I yelled. "It smells like sewage. Gordon, get ready. We can use that black goop to get Murray to tell us who he's working for."

Nabila, Ben, and Shane knelt down next to Director Z, helping him cough out some of the black nectar.

Gordon brought the squirming, squeeing splurtsar over to the struggling Murray. I shoved its trunk over Murray's mouth, but nothing happened.

The splurtsar struggled, shaking its head.

"He obeys no one but me," growled Murrayhotep.

"What do we do?" I asked.

Gordon squeezed the gross little space pig.

Nothing.

He slapped its pig butt.

It just SQUEED.

Murrayhotep laughed.

Gordon flipped it over onto its back.

I held the trunk tight and asked, "What are you doing?"

He jumped onto the pig, pushing his knees into its stomach.

SQUEEEEEEEBBBBLLLLUUUURRRRP!

I pinched Murray's nose as the black nectar came pouring out faster than before.

GULP.

And Murray stayed still.

I pulled the splurtsar's trunk away from Murray's drooling mouth, and Gordon rolled the splurtsar back over onto its stomach.

It stood up, took two steps, and crashed trunk-first into the moon rock, dead.

Long-Distance
Phone Call

"Director Z?!" I screamed, slapping his face. "Director Z!"

The black ooze that poured out of his mouth was now mixed with blood.

"Ugh," said Shane. "That doesn't look good."

Director Z writhed and moaned on the ground. He must have been in extreme pain. He coughed a mix of blood and black nectar onto my face.

"Oh man, I just wiped the other stuff off," I said, slowly starting the process again.

Director Z gave one last raspy breath and lay still.

"What? No!" I screamed. "This can't be happening."

"Should we do mouth-to-mouth?" asked Shane, leaning down.

"No, wait!" I yelled, pulling him back. "Listen." I put my ear directly over Director Z's mouth. "He's still breathing."

"Not for long, you fools," moaned Murray from beneath the werewolves. "You've killed the splurtsar, and your lame duck Director's only chance for survival."

"What do you mean?" Nabila asked.

Before he could answer, a strange jingling sound came from Director Z.

"What now?" I said. "Does Director Z have an alarm? Does this mean he's dying?"

"Oh, you don't need an alarm to tell you that," chuckled Murray.

"Shut it!" I yelled. "Just because you *can* tell the truth doesn't mean that you *have* to. Maybe we should fetch the witches. Grigore, can you go back and get Griselda?"

Grigore flapped back toward the ship. The jingling sound continued.

"It's his cell phone, you fools," laughed Murrayhotep. "And I hate you all."

"Okay, on second thought," said Shane, "keep telling the truth, Murray."

Shane and I leaned down over Director Z, pawing through the pockets of his perfectly pressed suit, which was stained with the black nectar. The stench of the dead splurtsar already filled the dank cave. I was worried Director Z would be next.

"Got it!" yelled Shane, and he pulled out a thin silver phone. "How's he even getting a signal on the moon?"

"Maybe it's communicating directly with the ship?" said Ben.

Shane flipped it open and said, "Um hello? Oh hi, Lunch Lady, how are you? Yes, I—"

"Gimme that!" I yelled, snatching the phone from Shane. "Lunch Lady, we have a situation."

"What is it?" she said. "We've been talkeeng with Deerector Z the entire trip, but he hadn't respondeed in so long, we decideed to risk calling. Is he . . ."

"Dying?" I said. "I think so. He was poisoned by a splurtsar."

"An overdose of splurtsar?" asked Lunch Lady. "Oh my. You must hurry. Geet the splurtsar and feed it some gassy food. Beans, cauleeflower, a turkey leg, anytheeng. Only the burp of a splurtsar can bring back the Deerector."

"We don't have any food," I said. "And we kind of killed the splurtsar."

"No!" she said over the phone. "Then I don't know what to do . . ."

There was a long pause.

"Lunch Lady," I said. "Are you still there? Director

Z's face is starting to turn blue."

"Okay," she said. "Wait. I have an idea: burpcessitation."

"Burpcessitation?" I asked.

"Burpcessitation," she confirmed. "You need to eat a little bit of the splurtsar. Well, maybe more than a little bit. You really need to bite off a few good chunks. Swallow it down fast, jump around, and then burp directly into the Deerector's mouth. Burp hard. Like you're doeeng mouth-to-mouth. Only you're pushing your burp into hees lungs. Hopefully the essence of splurtsar will combine with your digesteeve juices and create the appropriate antidote."

"This is crazy!" I yelled. "But his face is completely blue. I've gotta do it!"

"Then put the phone down and hurry!" yelled Lunch Lady. "Then let me know what happens."

I threw the phone down on the ground and ran over to the already-rotten corpse of the splurtsar.

"What do you have to do?" asked Gordon.

"No time," I yelled, grabbing the backside of the hairy, stinky little space creature, and taking a huge bite of his rump.

"Oh, that's just gross," said Ben. Despite being on the moon, and not in zero gravity, he vurped all over himself.

I choked back the rotten flesh and went in for

another bite, this one deeper and juicier. I could smell the dead splurtsar all over my mouth, in my nose, practically in my ears. Its blood stung a little. Its flesh tasted like a piece of chicken left out in the sun for a week.

"Mmmm, space bacon," chuckled Murrayhotep. "Nom, nom, nom!"

"We should give you black nectar more often," said Shane. "I like this new Murrayhotep."

"Zip it, kung fu weenie," said Murrayhotep.

I went for one last bite, just to be sure, this time hitting bone.

"Whatever you're gonna do, hurry!" screamed Nabila. "I can barely feel a pulse."

"I just need to jump around," I said, but because my mouth was filled with dead flesh, it came out, "Iush neeho shum-row."

I forced myself to swallow every last piece. My tongue searched around my mouth for any missing scraps. I gulped those down as well.

I jumped up and down on my way to Director Z. Lunch Lady was right—this was making me really gassy. In fact, now I was worried I would blow chunks directly into Director Z's mouth. I was starting to get stomach cramps, and the room was spinning.

My friends, who still had no idea what was going on, gathered around as I got on my knees, leaned down to Director Z's mouth, tried not to pass out, took a deep breath, and BUUUUUURRRRPPPPFFFFFFFFFFffffff!

I clamped my mouth down on Director Z's, burping the largest burp I had ever burped in my life directly into his lungs. His chest rose in front of me. I gave it all I had, pushing out every last bit of gas, and then for good measure, lifted my head, breathed in one more huge breath, and . . .

BRRRRRIIIIPPPPPPPFFFFFFffff!

I clamped my mouth down once again. Once I was sure I didn't have any more gas to give, I stood up, took two steps back, and passed out into Gordon's arms.

The last thing I remembered hearing was Murray saying, "To tell the truth, even I'm impressed."

Meet the
New Boss

When I woke up, Director Z was over me. This time, he was the one slapping me in the face.

He had the silver cell phone tucked under the crook of his neck.

"Yes, he's perfectly fine, Ms. Veracruz," he said calmly. "Yes, it was a close call. I will be eternally grateful . . . again. We'll speak again once we're on our way back to Earth, which should be shortly."

"Are you okay?" I asked Director Z, the smell of splurtsar still on my breath. My mouth felt fuzzy and tasted like I had licked Gordon's armpit after a big football game.

Griselda, who had finally made it to the cave, stood

next to Grigore. She saw me licking my pasty lips.

"It's okay, dearie," she said. "That will pass soon. I didn't pack the right herbs to help clear it up quicker."

Director Z held the phone down to me. "Yes, I've never felt better. Ms. Veracruz would like to speak with you," he said.

I grabbed the cell phone.

"Oh, Chrees!" yelled Lunch Lady. "You've saved the day once again. Those of us stuck on Earth, listening to everything all unfold, well, we're all so happy and proud of you."

"What do you mean, 'we'?" I asked. "Do you mean the Nurses?"

"Well, the Nurses, yes, and they do say hello, even though they're mad at you," said Lunch Lady. "But someone else has taken a special interest in your trip to space. Principal Prouty's grandfather is a resident of the Retirement Home."

"Whoa," I exclaimed. "No way!"

"What?" asked Shane, but Lunch Lady started talking again.

"Do you really think we'd be able to keep the huge secret of the five of you doeeng what you do at the Retirement Home without the help of the principal? What about all the work I've had to do to cover up the fact that you're on the moon? I've needed quite a bit of help. Your parents are more likely to believe lies from the principal, and it's much easier for her to administer the memory-eraser serum."

"Mr. Bradley's totally in on it, too, isn't he?" I asked. "His breath smells like one of his parents must be a zombie."

"Actually, Mr. Bradley—"

BLLLLLRRRZZZZZP!

"Hey!" I said to Director Z, handing him his phone. "She just cut out."

Director Z stared suspiciously down the tunnel. The glowing globes began to flicker in the cave. We could hear footsteps tramping toward us from deeper in the moon.

CLOMP CLOMP CLOMP.

The werewolves on top of Murray began to growl. Murrayhotep giggled with glee.

"Go!" Director Z commanded the vampire bats. "Warn the others."

"Warn the others about what?" I asked.

"He's coming to get you!" said Murrayhotep.

A dark hooded figure appeared in the tunnel, leading a dozen guards with huge spears, and whips made of electricity. One held an ax that broke into two sharp edges, curving in opposite directions.

The werewolves slowly backed off Murrayhotep, growling, as the hooded figure leaned down to pick up the mummy.

"Ah, Zorflogg!" said Murray. "It's not really all that great to see you. In fact, I must admit, you scare me to death. Here's a funny fact, when I was older—"

"There, there," said Zorflogg. "I knew that you were afraid of me from the first time you came to visit me and talk about how you were going to deceive all your friends." Zorflogg brushed a bit of moondust off Murray's shoulders. "Now, tell me something true that I don't know."

The mummy looked deep into Zorflogg's hood. I tried to see in, but all I could see were two glowing eyes. It was just too dark.

"Well, let's see," said Murrayhotep, scratching his chin. "I tried to kill the Director and blame it on the splurtsar. Yes, I think I was so occupied with that task that I didn't even see the werewolves when they jumped me. I'm dreadfully sorry about that, but what can I say?"

The mummy held his hands up in a sort of "what are you gonna do" way, while the guards closed Shane, Ben, Nabila, Gordon, Director Z, and me into a small circle. The werewolves bolted, and a few of the guards broke off to follow them.

"Let them go," yelled Zorflogg, and he held up a single gloved hand.

The guards obeyed.

"Now, let me be honest as well," Zorflogg said

ominously, "despite the fact that I haven't ingested any black nectar."

He walked closer to Murrayhotep and put both of his hands on Murrayhotep's shoulders. Murrayhotep shrank under the cold stare that came out of the hood.

"Let me be very, very honest," Zorflogg continued. "You have disappointed me very, very much. I've given you everything. Immunity. All the lebensplasm you'd want to drink. Not only did you try to kill this Director, but you failed so miserably that he is, in fact, now immune to black nectar. I've lost a prized splurtsar. You've proven yourself untrustworthy."

Murrayhotep whimpered. "Please . . . I . . ."

Zorflogg continued, "Let's see, what other truths can I bring up . . . Ah, yes. Fail me again and I shall destroy you utterly. Now get back to the mines and GET TO WORK!"

"I'm grateful that you haven't destroyed me, Master," said Murrayhotep. He hung his head and left the cave.

"Who are you?" Nabila said, defiantly stepping up to him. "What do you want?"

"I want it all," said Zorflogg, "but allow me to start with a snack."

Zorflogg picked up Nabila by her legs and flipped her upside down. Nabila squirmed and shook, trying to break free.

"Help!" she screamed. "Ben! Shane! Director Z!!!"

Give Me the Moon Juice!

We lunged forward to help Nabila, but two of the guards cracked their electric whips together, connecting them and forming an electric barrier.

"Aaaaaahhh!" Nabila's screams echoed through the cave.

We watched helplessly as Zorflogg slowly brought Nabila's feet toward his head. With a slimy hiss, a black tongue emerged from the shadows of the hood and licked the bottom of her shoes.

"WHAT. IS. HE. DOOOOING?" Nabila screeched, her face red from being hung upside down.

The tongue retreated into the hood with a SLURP, and a great MMMMMMM echoed through the caves, shaking moondust off the cave ceiling.

Without warning, he swung Nabila over the electric barrier directly at us.

"GRRRWAAAAH! OOF!"

We cushioned her fall and crashed down like a heap of scared bowling pins.

"Such a paltry treat," said Zorflogg, "but enjoyable nonetheless. I noticed that the deep grooves in her sporty sneakers collected a fair amount of lebensplasm from walking through this newly formed moon chasm. Sometimes I like to enjoy it unrefined. Frivolous, I know. I cannot wait to mine this newly found section."

"That would explain the moon muck," said Shane.

"You're mining lebensplasm?" Ben asked. "What for?"

"So he can drain the moon—the original monster and the source of all the Earth's lebensplasm," said Director Z.

"The moon's a monster?" I asked.

But Director Z continued, talking directly at the hooded figure.

"Then, once you've destroyed the moon, you'll take all the pendants to solidify your hold over the Earth and all its inhabitants. Isn't that true, Cordoba?"

"Don't make me tell you again, you powerless fool, Cordoba is dead. I am Zorflogg! And, yes, the world shall be MINE."

He grabbed Director Z by his neck and lifted his head up into the ceiling of the moon cave, crunching his head against moon rock.

"I don't believe it," said Director Z, spitting his words out through Zorflogg's grip. "You were a terrible Director—you couldn't even control your Retirement Home! How dare you think you could control the Earth? Especially in your corrupt state—drunk off the power of lebensplasm."

"You were a Director?" I asked. "A Director who drank monster juice?"

"Yes, he was the first and only half-human, half-monster Director," Director Z said, his face turning red as he tried to pull the massive gloved hands off his throat. "But he grew corrupt, trying and failing to use the monsters under his charge to take over the world. He grew his strength by ingesting monster juice—"

"Oh, now you're calling it monster juice?" laughed Zorflogg. "What a delightful little joke for the kids."

". . . too much monster juice for his human side to handle," Director Z continued. "For a human to drink monster juice more than once, though it would give him much strength, would most certainly be fatal. The overdose of juice literally melted both parts together— the rotten, dead human side with the evil, monstrous monster side—and now he must drink monster juice to survive. That is his real reason for draining the moon.

How foolish the other Directors and I were to banish him to space. We never thought he could unlock the secret of the moon."

"Silence, you fool!" yelled Zorflogg, and he flung Director Z down onto the ground. "It is true that at first, I merely needed the monster juice for me, to keep myself alive. But now I see that it is the key to a new monsterdom on Earth. I would kill you if it were not for the knowledge that you possess. No, I won't make the same mistake that brainless mummy almost made. Guards! Take him back to my throne room! Prepare the zapeel! We must work even harder now that my precious splurtsar has perished."

Two guards stepped forward to grab Director Z.

"Don't touch him!" yelled Gordon, and he jumped forward to protect Director Z. He was blocked with a great ZAPPPPP!

And he flew onto the ground.

"Gordon!" I yelled.

Shane got into a karate pose.

"We can't fight them!" I said, pushing Shane back. Then I added in a whisper, "Not now. Not yet."

As the guards dragged Z away, he gave me a little wink and a smile.

"What Chris says is true," said Zorflogg. "No one can fight my new breed. Not without facing certain death."

We helped Gordon to his feet and brushed the moondust off his shoulders.

"New breed?" mumbled Gordon. "What new breed?"

"Since the beginning of time, the world has always had Retirement Homes for monsters," said Zorflogg. "When enough people forget about the monsters that once frightened them, they lose their power. With the invention of movies and the Internet, everyone was convinced that monsters were just made up. Creations. They just couldn't exist. But we were real—and we were losing our powers. Some had become so weak that they were withering away into nothingness. Monsterdom would soon fall."

"If you're so concerned about monsterdom, then why are you trying to destroy it?" I asked.

"Because the monsters of old proved to me they are too weak. I tried to get the old monsters under my direction to rise up and control the Earth as was our birthright. But they failed me. And I'm glad they failed me. When your Director and the other Directors banished me to space, it was here, on the moon, that I realized monsterdom needed a fresh start, with a new breed, and a new set of rules."

"What makes you think you'll be able to take over the world?" asked Nabila.

"Thanks to the Tentacled Heads of Andromeda," said Zorflogg, "I have power beyond my wildest dreams."

"The tentacled heads of what now?" asked Gordon.

Zorflogg turned swiftly to Gordon, "Oh, you're familiar with them, most certainly. They've already dined on one of your friends."

Zorflogg clapped his hands, and the unmistakable sound of wet burps echoed down the tunnel. But they were different somehow. The smell of vurp filled the room.

"Oh man," said Ben. "If that's what I smelled like on the ship, I'm so sorry."

"Nope . . . nope," coughed Shane. "This is so much worse."

A dozen of them entered the cave, floating inside the moon just as they had in zero gravity. We tried to dodge them as they floated past, but their writhing tentacles reached out and with a POP POP POP left little red marks on our cheeks.

They surrounded Zorflogg, and he greeted them. "Oh, my dear, dear friends!" he said. Their tentacles gently stroked him, and he purred like a cat.

"When I saw them here, on the moon," he said, "I knew I had found the perfect creature. They were the only beings I had ever seen capable of absorbing lebensplasm and depositing it back. They regurgitated *pure* lebensplasm. I provoked them, feeding off the delicious cloud of lebensplasm they attacked me with, and soon they were tamed, and their DNA is now in every one of my creations. They began to call me 'Zorflogg' in their native tongue, and since they have shown me my new, true power, I knew I must take the new, true name they gave me."

"But what does the moon have to do with this?" asked Nabila.

"Once the moon falls, I'll have the Earth in my grasp, and my new breed will rule!" Zorflogg said.

"Wait," said Shane. "If the moon falls, won't it crash into the Earth and obliterate everyone there?"

"Young fool, I don't actually mean that it will fall." Zorflogg was perturbed. "I meant I would defeat it. You know . . . FALL. In that sense."

"Well, I for one think you should have been more specific," said Shane.

"SILENCE!" yelled Zorflogg.

"Yeah, silence, dude," Ben said, shuddering.

"I will give you one chance, and once chance only, to join me," said Zorflogg. "You all seem so fresh, so smart. You made it all the way up to the moon, and I'm sure that those worthless monsters didn't help you. It would be a pity to have to enslave you along with those old fossils. Join me! Join me in my laboratory and let me make you the first humans to carry the Andromedan gene. When the time comes to take over the Earth, you can convince your fellow humans to make the same choice."

I stepped up to Zorflogg defiantly. "Absolutely not!" I yelled.

My friends stepped behind me. "No way!" they said.

"Well, that is a deeply unfortunate choice on your part. For I won't stop until I change the fate of monsterdom forever."

"I'd like to see you try!" yelled Gordon.

"Instead of accepting my invitation, you and your irrelevant monster friends will see nothing but the deepest, darkest recesses of the moon for the rest of your days," Zorflogg announced. "You shall be my slaves, forced to work an eternity in my mines, which are staffed by all my failed creations, doomed to crush and purify moon rocks into monster juice."

Zorflogg clapped his hands, and guards came forward to grab my friends and drag them away.

"Where are they taking them?" I asked.

"To the mines, where their eternal work begins," he said. "And you, too, shall join them. But first there is something of mine you possess, and I shall take it from you."

His hand, cold even through the thick black gloves he wore, wrapped around my wrist, and he dragged me deeper into the moon.

Doomed!

"Chris, I would ask you to consider joining me," said Zorflogg, his voice echoing around his throne room. "I've heard much from Murray about you and the way you almost foiled his plan. Well done."

As Zorflogg headed to the massive throne, chiseled out of moon rock, I could see that he wasn't walking so much as floating. He folded the bottom half of his robes, spun around, and came to a rest on the seat. The throne began to glow the same green as the globes of light we had seen in the tunnel.

"The way I see it, you have two choices," said Zorflogg from the comfort of his chair. "Join me as a top-ranking lieutenant and assist me in taking over your pitiful world. I also know from Murray your love for space. I'm quite sorry to ruin your moon trip, but I could certainly, once all of the taking-over-the-world business is done, promise that my friends from Andromeda would take you on a tour of their home galaxy."

"What's my second choice?" I asked.

"Slavery and death."

"That sounds fine to me," I said, though it didn't sound fine at all. It actually sounded quite terrible.

Zorflogg sighed from his throne and floated over to me once again. His cold hand lay over the pendant that I wore under my shirt.

"Then again," hissed Zorflogg, his sour breath pouring all over my face, "perhaps you aren't as smart as I thought. You did, after all, bring this pendant directly to me."

He reached into my shirt through my collar, and I shivered.

With a quick snap, he pulled the pendant off and held it up in the light.

"Wait a minute . . . ," he growled, tilting it so that the light from the giant globe that hung in the center of the throne room shone through it.

"Is there a problem?" I asked.

"There most certainly is," yelled Zorflogg, "This is another *fake*! But how? It must be on the ship. There is absolutely no way you could have made it to the moon without its power driving the monsters along."

"You are correct," I said. "There is absolutely no way I could have gotten the monsters to do what I needed them to do without the power of the pendant. But once we were in the moon's orbit, I jettisoned the pendant into deep space. It nearly cost us our lives, because I certainly could have used the power during the landing. But now it's out there in space. Better get your little Andromedan doggies to go fetch! Now who's the fool?"

"How DARE you!" he yelled. "To the mines with you! Do my bidding, slave!"

With two powerful claps, he summoned two powerful guards, who dragged me out of the room.

We stood in a massive cave deep in the moon, crude tools in our hands. We awaited our "trainer," who would give us instruction on the kind of work we would be doing until the end of our days.

"But I saw you command the monsters *after* we got off the ship," whispered Shane. "So I know you still have the pendant."

"Well, you know that, and I know that, but thank goodness, Zorflogg doesn't know that," I replied.

"How'd you do it?" asked Gordon. "You know . . . convince him."

"I just insulted him," I said. "I knew that if I made him feel stupid, he would be too angry to see that I was actually tricking him."

"Good tactic," said Nabila. "So, where is it?"

"Somewhere safe," I said. "Somewhere I hope Zorflogg doesn't think to look. I've already told you all too much. It puts you in danger."

My friends looked at me, waiting for me to tell them where I had hidden it, but it was the one secret I had to keep deep inside myself.

The cave we were in was so large that there was barely any echo. Through the eerie silence, a troop of guards hauled in all the monsters who had been pulled off the ship.

The monsters were lined up behind us, ready for what we were told would be "training." Around us, in fields of boulders, strange creatures tapped away at the moon rocks with different odd-looking instruments. Occasionally, someone (or rather, something) would roll up with a wheelbarrow to cart off the moon rocks to a massive machine that crushed them. Everyone looked exhausted and miserable.

"Is that Murrayhotep?" asked Shane. He pointed behind a small mound of moon rock on the other side of the massive cave. Two small furry and fanged creatures were working at the moon rock, chipping away at it slowly. Another creature that looked like an anteater with wings waddled over to the fallen moon rock to snorf it up.

"I think so . . . ," I said.

Murrayhotep pulled out a small glass vial of green, sinister-looking fluid.

"Monster juice," I said. "It must be the daily ration that Zorflogg gives him for having betrayed us."

Murrayhotep drank the bottle down greedily, his red tongue flitting around inside the bottle to lick up every last bit.

"Ew," said Nabila.

Murrayhotep got up, wiped off some moondust, and straightened his bandages. He started to walk toward us, but then suddenly, with a smack of his lips, walked back and crouched behind the rocks once more.

"He's going to have another bottle!" Gordon said. "That greedy old fart."

"Maybe he needs a little extra after the splurtsar attack?" Shane wondered.

We watched as Murrayhotep practically inhaled the second bottle.

"No, I think he's just . . . ," I started.

"Addicted," Ben finished. "Now, quiet, he's walking right for us."

Murray walked toward us, but not in a completely straight line. He sort of zigged and zagged.

He almost stumbled when he stopped in front of us.

"I think he acts even older with the monster juice," Gordon said, snickering.

Murray straightened up right away, his eyes going from unfocused to focused in a snap.

"Keep your trap shut, you sssniveling little sssnot," he said.

With that, Murray pulled a huge whip out from under his bandages and held it high.

"He's still slurring his words," Nabila whispered to Ben.

"You too, Nabila!" snapped Murray. "This issssn't a game. You're a slave in a moon mine! I'm your bossssss now. And don't ssschtink I forgot about that time you unraveled my wrappingssss!"

He brought the whip up over his head, and I instinctively jumped in front of Nabila, waiting for the blow.

Twenty-Three

"I've been wanting to do this for a long time," growled Murrayhotep.

I crouched and cowered, waiting for the whip to come snapping down on me.

"Let's not be too hasty, Mister Mummy."

"Back off, Twenty-Three!"

"Huh?" I said, and turned around. A small green creature stood between Murray and me. The creature was toddler-size, and looked sort of like a lizard crossed with a tabby cat. Stripes of fur crisscrossed his scaly body.

"Zorflogg said to train these humans in the next three hours, and that's what I intend to do," the small green creature said. "I think that's what you should help me do, as well—if I were you, I'd want to do exactly what Zorflogg said. You're already on his bad side after the stunt you pulled with the splurtsar."

Murray looked at the small creature for a moment longer and then lowered his whip.

"You heard Zorflogg," Murray said. "Three hours! Better get to crackin'!"

Murray snapped the whip right at the small green creature's feet.

"Ha-ha-ha!" The small green creature laughed. "Get to crackin'. I get it, I get it . . ."

Murray headed off, and the small green creature stepped in front of us and raised his hands to get everyone's attention.

"Hello?" he said. "Hello, all! My name is Twenty-Three, and I'll be training you on the proper procedure for the extraction and refinement of lebensplasm from moon rock."

A few of the monsters moaned, "Hello, Twenty-Three."

"Now, most of the creatures I train have to start from scratch since they were only recently created by Master Zorflogg," Twenty-Three continued. "But I'm sure you guys bring a little more to the table. Everyone knows what a moon rock is, correct?"

There was a general rumble of "yes," "yeah," and

"um, I think so" from the crowd.

"Okay, great!" said Twenty-Three. "And I'm sure everyone knows what a pickax is, correct?"

Again came moans of "yes" from the crowd.

"Wonderful," said Twenty-Three. "Let's get started."

Twenty-Three gave us the entire rundown of the process behind collecting and processing moon rock: breaking it into the right-size pieces, collecting it for the crushing machine, having it crushed and then boiled into the proper concentration. He showed us how to use pickaxes, tongs for the sharper pieces of rock, and our masks, which were needed for the extrafine moondust.

"Okay, well, you were a really great group, and I really appreciate that you paid attention to everything I had to say today," said Twenty-Three at the end of his training. "Does anyone have any questions?"

"Yeah," Gordon whispered to me. "Why is he so happy?"

"I think he's the only guy more excited than Chris to be on the moon," Shane whispered back.

The crowd of monsters started shuffling away to different parts of the cave.

"You know how much I wanted to surround myself with amazing moon rock," I whispered. "But not like this . . ."

"Did you have a question, guys?" Twenty-Three asked, walking over to us. "If not, you should probably get to work. Zorflogg isn't a big fan of idle chatter. He runs a professional moon, that guy."

He flashed us a big, lizardy smile.

"Okay, I've got one," said Nabila. "Where does all the moon rock go once it's crushed? You know, for refining?"

"Oh, wonderful question, earthling," replied Twenty-Three. He rubbed his scaly hands together, so excited to answer the question. "The crushed moon rock is vacuumed into processing vats in the next cave over. Very high security over there—even I'm not allowed. And I don't blame them—I would totally sneak a drink of the high-powered stuff."

"Why is your name Twenty-Three?" I asked.

"That's sort of a long story," said Twenty-Three, looking around for Murrayhotep or any of Zorflogg's other guards. "Are you guys familiar with the sangala creatures Zorflogg created?"

"Yes," Nabila said. "We were plagued by them just before we took off for the moon. Disgusting things. Terrible things."

"Well, I am one," said Twenty-Three.

"What?" Nabila asked. "Oh, I'm so sorry. If I had known . . . I mean, you don't look like a sangala."

"That's okay," said Twenty-Three. "I don't like the final versions, either. You see, I was version twenty-three of the sangala, which is how I got my name."

"Version twenty-three?" asked Shane. "What do you mean?"

"It's hard work perfecting the DNA splicing and biology of creating new creatures," said Twenty-Three. "Some of Zorflogg's creations were relatively easy to make. Sussuroblats were a breeze. And the membranium already existed—Zorflogg just needed to modify them slightly. I've heard rumors that the scientists have even made the skin better since then. The sangala, however, was a tough creature to make. They had to look like cats or dogs as they absorbed monster juice, all the while hiding a reptilian gene that could explode forth at any moment. It took Zorflogg twenty-four tries to get the sangala right. I was the twenty-third try, and the first to result in a living creature."

"Oh right," said Shane. "Yeah, I can see how you could be a sangala now. The mix of cat and lizard. The sharp teeth. Except, you're so nice. And so smart."

"Exactly," said Twenty-Three. "Which is why I was rejected. Aside from the fact that the lizard part of me was already showing, Zorflogg couldn't send hundreds of friendly creatures out to collect monster juice—the worst damage I could do was talk the old monsters to death with intelligent-but-boring conversation. So he kept me on the moon, doomed for all eternity to work the mines, just like you guys. And just like all the other rejected creations."

"So why are you still so happy?" asked Gordon.

"I guess it's just in my nature," replied Twenty-Three. "I must have the happy gene in my DNA. Plus, I'm a trainer, not a laborer. And I get all sorts of tasty grubs to eat from Zorflogg. I mix them with cat treats. Yum!"

"Yeah, that sounds delicious," said Ben with a burp.

"But I guess I'm okay because I know that this is all going to end soon," said Twenty-Three.

"What do you mean?" I asked.

"Well, the mines won't be open much longer," said Twenty-Three. "The Andromedans have always been here, hiding on the dark side of the moon, attracted by its lebensplasm. It gives them energy, but they could never figure out how to drain the moon's lebensplasm directly. Now Zorflogg is working on figuring it out for them. And when that happens, then it's all over—SLURP!—and done . . . and then I hope to finally visit Earth."

"Yeah," said Gordon, "it will be great to see all the screaming and explosions and violence and destruction when Zorflogg's minions take over the world. Just peachy."

"Well," said Twenty-Three, slapping Gordon on the back of the leg, "I, for one, will be happy for the change. All right, guys, better get to work. It was great talking with you!"

"I guess he really does have the happy gene," I said. "Totally creepy."

"Well, at least we made a friend," said Shane. "Someone to help us out. Someone to show us the ropes and teach us things. Now we know what Zorflogg meant by 'when the moon falls' . . ."

"I, for one, hope that we won't be here long enough to need help," I said. "We've got to think of a way out of this situation."

Twenty-Three walked away and Murrayhotep rushed up to us, whip raised high.

"Get moving, you worms," Murrayhotep said. "Or this time, you will taste my whip!"

Moon-Mine Blues

Four hours later, it felt like we had been on the moon for a hundred years.

"Maybe Twenty-Three was right," Shane huffed. "We should be happy that we won't have to do this forever. Let's hope Zorflogg teaches the Andromedans to drink monster juice soon."

"And then what?" asked Nabila. "We'll be doomed to do something else terrible for all of eternity. Like crush poor old monsters into pulp. At least Ben is finally getting in shape. I've been trying everything I can to get him to build a little muscle mass."

"Aw, shucks," Ben said, blushing and crushing another rock proudly. "That makes this whole doomed-to-die-on-the-moon thing worth it."

"You know, it wouldn't be too bad to have a little Andromedan DNA," Gordon said, chipping away at the moon rock. "I mean, I was a sussuroblat for a while, and it wasn't too terrible. I certainly didn't have to mine moon rock all day long."

"No way," I said, bringing my pick down on the next rock with a SHCRACK. "We can't give up. Plus, I don't think the offer is on the table anymore. Zorflogg is too mad with me after I rubbed in the fake pendant."

Murrayhotep stood up from the outcropping of moon rock he was sitting on and yelled, "Less talking, more mining."

A knee-high creature pulling a wagon approached to collect our stones. His skin was gray and wrinkled like an elephant's, but he had the pink nose of a pig. Every time he snorfed, a little bit of black goo sprayed out.

"A failed splurtsar," I said, and patted him on the head. "Which number are you? Do you have the happy gene?"

The little guy just snorfed again and moved along.

Once we had filled the wagon with rocks, I looked up to see that Murrayhotep had left his post.

"He's off to drink another bottle!" I said, dropping behind the mound of moon boulders I was working on. "Guys, gather around, quick!"

My friends dropped their pickaxes and rushed over.

"I've been brewing up a crazy idea," I said. "But I think it's the only way to get out of here."

"What is it?" Shane asked.

"We drink the monster juice," I replied.

Everyone stared at me like I had an arm growing out of my head.

"We drink the *what* now?" asked Gordon.

"The monster juice," I said confidently. "We drink the monster juice."

"But how?" Nabila asked. "You heard Twenty-Three: The refined monster juice is in another heavily guarded cave."

Gordon shook his head. "Forget 'how,' let's talk about why. This doesn't sound like the best idea."

"Not to mention," said Ben, making a retching sound, "how am I going to keep it down?"

"This is crazy," said Nabila. "Director Z said that it could kill us."

Gordon nodded in agreement.

"I like crazy," said Shane. "Plus, Director Z only said that using it more than once could kill us. Which makes me think that using it once would be okay. Tell us more, Chris."

I looked up to make sure Murrayhotep wasn't on the way back from his juice break.

"This is what I'm thinking," I said. "We're young humans, and won't need to drink too much monster juice to feel an effect. We could share one of Murrayhotep's bottles."

"What do you think it will do to us?" Ben asked.

"I hope it transforms me into a werewolf," said Shane. "I think I'd make an awesome werewolf. Karatewerewolf!"

"I have no idea," I replied. "But I'm sure it will make us powerful. Powerful enough to fight through whatever comes our way."

"Will we be invincible?" asked Nabila.

"I don't know," I said. "I just know we'll be more powerful than we are now. Hopefully powerful enough to fight our way into the secure section that contains all the pure monster juice. Then we let all our monsters feast on the supply, destroy Zorflogg, and get the heck off the moon."

"What if it doesn't work?" asked Gordon. "What if it just makes us sick? What if it works differently for kids? What if we d—"

"Look, I'm not going to force anyone to do it who doesn't want to do it," I said. "I'd love to just have the monsters drink the monster juice, but they need too much, and we might not have enough time to hatch a plan like that. Does anyone else have a better idea?"

"I'm in," said Shane.

"Me too, I guess," said Ben, who retched again.

"I can't think of anything better," said Nabila.

"Okay," said Gordon. "What do we need to do?"

"We need to create a distraction," I said. "Something that will keep Murrayhotep so busy that he won't notice when we snag a bottle of monster juice from his wrappings."

"Ooooh," said Shane. "I think I've got a good one. We need to talk to the werewolves."

"You and the werewolves! How are they going to help?" I asked. "They can't howl anymore. They've got muzzles when they're in dog form."

"You keep talking and I'll put a muzzle on *you*!" said Murrayhotep, who was back on his outcropping of rocks, watching us.

"We'll have to figure this out later," I whispered. "You *know* he's gonna take another break."

"Let's hope he doesn't drink all of it," Ben said.

"Shut it!" yelled Murrayhotep. "Get to work!"

"I feel bad for Frederick," said Shane. "He has no idea, does he?"

"No idea whatsoever," I replied, perfectly cracking into a moon rock with my pick. "Hey, I'm getting pretty good at this."

"We couldn't risk letting Frederick know the plan," said Nabila. "He might not have gone along with—"

"Shhhh!" said Ben. "It's Murrayhotep!"

Murrayhotep walked up to Gordon, who was slamming a large rock down onto a smaller one.

"Don't do it like that, you dimwit!" growled Murrayhotep. "You've got to use your pick, or all the juice crystals will be ruined."

"Man, I can smell the monster juice on his breath all the way over here," Ben whispered to me.

"You most certainly can," said Murrayhotep, quickly turning toward Ben. "And all that delicious lebensplasm has given me sharp senses—including my sense of hearing. So keep your lips sealed, or I'll come over there and sew them shut."

Behind Murrayhotep, Pietro and Howie started to rub their ragged, overgrown sideburns swiftly.

Knowing that Murrayhotep was listening closely, I looked at my friends and squinted, hoping they knew I was saying "get ready!"

Frederick was busily crushing rock with his bare hands, sending showers of monster-juice crystals everywhere. (Murrayhotep would not be pleased.)

The werewolves crept up on him from behind, and . . .

ZAAAAPP!

"Gaaah!" screamed Frederick.

The werewolves began rubbing their muttonchops again. Howie took off his shirt, exposing his hairy back.

Pietro rubbed Howie's back furiously, and sparks jumped off the hair that stood up on the top of the werewolves' heads.

"Stop it, guys," said Frederick. "Please don't."

Murrayhotep turned his attention away from Ben and toward the giggling werewolves.

"Knock it off!" yelled Murrayhotep.

But it was too late.

"Here I come," yelled Pietro. "I'm comin' ta getcha!"

ZAAAAAAAAAAPPPPPPPP!

Frederick shot up so high that his head got stuck in a crevice in the ceiling of the moon cave.

Murrayhotep ran to grab the werewolves, but they transformed into muzzled wolves and ran around—and in between—his legs.

"Okay," I said. "Now's my chance. Get ready! We're going to have to guzzle it down quickly."

I ran up to Murrayhotep, who was half bent over, trying to stop the werewolves. I saw two bottles sticking out of the wrappings on either side of his butt. I snatched them both and ran back to my friends.

"Hurry!" I said.

I passed Shane one bottle and pulled the cork out of the other.

GULP!

"Ugh," I said while passing it to Ben. "I feel like spiders are crawling around in my stomach."

"You didn't have to tell me that," yelled Ben, and he GULPED. He retched almost immediately.

"Hold it in," yelled Gordon, and he GULPED.

I looked over to see if Shane and Nabila had finished their bottle.

That's when I heard Murrayhotep yell, "What do you think you're doing?"

Monster Juice Madness

Now, as a kid, my instinct would have been to cower in front of Murrayhotep in fear, saying, "Sorry, sorry, sorry."

But I wasn't just a kid anymore.

Instead of opening my mouth to say sorry, I opened a mouth full of fangs and let out a "BRWAAAAARRRGH!"

Murrayhotep's eyes bugged out of his head. He backed off, tripping over a moon rock, and knocked himself out.

I panted, feeling the power of the monster juice coursing through my veins. I looked over at the others. Ben had turned a shade of green, but not because he was sick.

"I've got webbed hands," Ben said, staring at the new green flesh between his fingers. "Swamp creature." He reached up to feel his gills.

"Aw, fang it!" Shane said. "I mean, I really wanted werewolf, but vampire feels pretty good." He licked his teeth. "I vant to suck your blooood."

"Uggghhh," said Nabila. "Urrggh."

"Zombie?" asked Ben.

"She'll eventually learn how to talk," said Shane.

Nabila turned to him with a blank expression. She cocked her head and said, "Brains?"

"See?" said Shane.

"Uggghhh," said Gordon. He was crumpled up on the floor.

"Looks like Gordon got zombie, too," Ben said.

"Noooo," Gordon said. "It made me so sick. Ugh, my stomach."

I padded over to Gordon and pushed my muzzle into his side to try to get him to roll over.

"Chris," said Gordon, still clutching his stomach, "get this dog off me."

I was about to ask, "What dog?" when I realized he was talking about me.

I was a werewolf.

"AROOOOOOO!" I howled. It felt amazing.

The cave shook, and Frederick fell out of the ceiling.

"Thanks," he moaned.

"Awesome!" yelled Shane.

Murrayhotep was awoken from his stupor, and popped his head up in disbelief, staring at us again.

The other slaves and their guards took notice, and once the shaking stopped, they all stared at us in silence, wondering what was going to happen next.

Nabila took one look at Murrayhotep and bolted toward him, her arms outstretched, drooling, her glasses tilted awkwardly on her nose.

"Braaaaaaaiins," she yelled.

"Okay, forget what I said on the spaceship, now *that's* the fastest zombie I've ever seen," said Shane.

"Guuaaaaaaaaarrds," yelled Murrayhotep, and he scrambled up to run.

I barked at Shane, whose job it was to relay the plan.

"Residents," he yelled, his vampire voice carrying through the cave. "We're going to take the secure section, that contains the pure monster juice—"

I barked at Shane again.

"I mean the pure lebensplasm," he continued. "Those who are not residents, help us and you will be accepted into our monstrous ranks. We will not hesitate to destroy you if you stand in our way."

All the slaves, our old friends and our new friends, threw their tools to the side and rushed to the doors that led to the secure monster-juice holding area. We rushed to join them as they pounded on the doors.

Before we could even get our footing, the huge iron doors blasted open. Guards in black hooded capes poured in on foot. Above . . .

"Andromedans!" Ben yelled.

Instinctively, I jumped up and, with my powerful werewolf jaws, grabbed the tentacles of one of the Andromedans. The sound of the crunch sent excitement through my furry body. I swallowed a bit of the disgusting blood and enjoyed the feeling. I flailed my head around to pull the Andromedan down onto the dirty moon-rock floor. It hit with a thud, sending a ripple through its disgustingly swollen skin. The zombies, still angered by the loss of their friend, approached it and began ripping into the bulbous head.

I took down another and another. My muzzle was wet with green Andromedan blood, and I licked my lips, panting with hunger and excitement.

Shane turned into a vampire bat and flew directly into the Andromedans' heads, breaking the huge, zit-like bulges on the top and spraying the monsters below with delicious juices. Not a lot, but enough to get them excited. Zombies swiped. Vampires snarled. One banshee screamed at just the right volume and pitch, and one of the Andromedans exploded, sending a waterfall of monster juice down.

"Waaaahoooo," screeched Bat Shane, tickling my sensitive werewolf ears.

Ben and Nabila were swiping away at the guards, who were charging in two by two. Ben was using his webbed hands to deflect electric charges with ease, and his scaly skin was protecting him from the massive axes, and occasional bites from Nabila, who was chomping in every direction.

I could see giant tanks of monster juice through the doors. We pushed ever closer, the monsters getting excited to see the bounty ahead.

"Make a push for it!" yelled Ben. "Come on, everyone. Once we get into that room, you'll be bathing in monster juice."

"Not quite so fast," yelled Zorflogg as he flew through the doors with dozens more Andromedans.

Shane landed next to me and POPPED back into his human form.

"Whew," he said. "Flying takes it out of me, I gotta say."

I barked in the direction of Zorflogg.

"Oh, I didn't see you come in, Mr. Zorflogg," said Shane.

Even Nabila knew that was a brain she was incapable of chewing on. We stood face-to-face with Zorflogg and his floating heads. Nobody knew who was going to make the first move.

The cave was once again silent. Then, from the corner, Gordon said, "Mommy, I want to go home. I ate too many corn dogs and I think I'm going to throw up."

I had forgotten about Gordon.

Zorflogg pointed to our sad, sick friend and commanded, "Destroy him!"

The Andromedans flew toward Gordon, and we followed as quickly as we could, Shane once again frantically biting and scratching their faces to slow them down.

But there were too many.

As we reached Gordon, I jumped up to grab tentacle after tentacle. Shane, Ben, and Nabila formed a protective circle around Gordon, pushing back any guard that approached, while helping me with the Andromedans.

Shane jumped up and sank his teeth into one of the Andromedans. A SCHLUCKING sound could be heard as he drained it dry.

"Stop!" Nabila yelled at Shane. "You can't drink monster juice a second time! You'll die!"

I called to Shane to stop, but all that came out was a loud howl.

Everyone turned to watch as Shane drained the Andromedan of a giant mouthful of monster juice.

His eyes grew wide and his head shook briefly before he turned to us and smiled.

"Man, that was refreshing!" he said.

"Huh," Ben said, struggling with a tentacle. "Maybe it didn't harm him because he's in monster mode. I'm still not going to risk a second sip."

We continued to push off the attack as best as we could, and it was all going very well, until the Andromedans started vurping.

"I'm starting to feel really light-headed," said Shane.

"They're starting to absorb our monster juice!" I yelled, suddenly in human form once again.

"Thank goodness I can talk again," said Nabila. "Wait, I can talk again! Did I eat any brains? Please tell me I didn't eat any brains!"

"Forget about your brains," I yelled. "Everyone, we have to push harder or we're done for!"

But the other monsters were weakened by the vurping and started falling over and flailing about, like roaches after a hit of Raid.

BURP BLIP BLURP.

The Andromedans kept burping their acidic vurps.

"Oh gross," said Gordon. "The burping is making me totally sick."

"Maybe *you* should try burping," said Ben. "That's always helped me."

Gordon continued to writhe in agony while trying to force a belch out of himself. The harder he pushed, the more his body convulsed. His stomach started pulsating madly. I was sure that an alien would pop out at any second. The shaking got worse as the throbbing mass moved from his stomach and started working its way up toward his mouth.

"Watch out!" Shane yelled as he covered his face. "Something's coming out, and I bet it's going to be grossmazing."

Gordon's eyes opened wide as his whole body lifted off the cave floor. His mouth flew open wider than any mouth should be able to. That's when it happened.

BLUUUUUUUUUUUUUUUUUUUURPUH!

From somewhere deep inside Gordon came the most moon-shaking, neighbor-waking burp known to mankind . . . or moonkind. I was pretty sure that, despite the fact that it was 250,000 miles away, people could hear it on Earth. It was that epic.

And it stank worse than anything imaginable. Like rotten eggs on a summer day times a million.

A tunnel shook open behind us. And for a moment, the Andromedans pulled back. Gordon's burp made them too stunned to vurp anymore.

"Go, hurry," Shane commanded, covering his nose and moving monsters quickly through the newly formed crack and into the cave beyond.

We held our ground at the beginning, but were soon failing.

"We just have to retreat!" I yelled.

Ben and Nabila followed the monsters. Gordon

swayed in front of the Andromedans, relieved and stunned from his burp.

BLURP BURRRP BRAAAP.

"Gordon," I yelled, rushing up to him. "We have to go! We've got to get into the new cave as quickly as we can. The Andromedans have recovered!"

Shane and I each put a shoulder under Gordon's arms and rushed away from the Andromedans into the narrow passage to the next cave.

"Gah!" Shane yelled as an Andromedan tentacle snagged his leg.

"Shane!" I yelled. "SHANE!" I was able to grab his arm, but I had to drop Gordon to do it. He fell to the floor with an OOOOOOF.

I used both hands to pull Shane toward me, but my grip was slipping.

BLURP BURRRP BRAAAP.

A green cloud settled itself around my head. It smelled like a thousand babies had spit up dog barf all over my face.

"Gordon," I growled, the last of my werewolf strength leaving me. "Go get somebody to help. I can't hold on much longer. The vurps! I'm getting so weak. I'm not even a werewolf anymore!"

I looked back into the cave, and yelled, "HELP!"

Gordon slowly made his way to his feet, clawing at moon rock to rise and face the Andromedans.

"It's time to fight burps with burps," sputtered Gordon. "Let's do this."

He sucked in the air like a huge vacuum, rumbling and vibrating as he did it. The moon rock around us trembled as he cleared the air of all of the vurp. His eyes watered as he inhaled and inhaled, his face turning blue, a great PPPPPPRRRRUUUUBBBB sound resonating from his body.

The Andromedans began to retreat. They dropped Shane, and he landed directly on top of me. I tried to push him off.

"Wait, we might want to stay down," he said. "This is going to be awesome."

For a few seconds there was complete silence. From deep in the cave, a witch yelled, "What's going on?"

I looked up at Gordon. He shook in place, his eyes bugging. He slowly opened his mouth.

BRRRRRAAAAAAAAPPPPPPGGGLLLLL.

The green spew of the Andromedans was blown back into their faces.

GGGGGGGLLLLLLAAAAARRRRRP.

Gordon kept going. The Andomedans screeched terribly as they flew backward into the cave.

PPPPPPRRRRRRUUUUUPPPP.

Gordon stopped for a second, took in one last quick breath, and—

BURP!

—sent one last insanely loud thunderclap of a burp through the bodies of the Andromedans.

Every single Andromedan head exploded into a fiery, fleshy, chunky shower of green, green, and more green.

"Yeah!" I screamed.

But before I could high-five Gordon, the passageway crumbled around us.

Out of the
Frying Pan . . . .

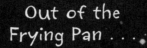

Gordon lunged forward and scooped up Shane and me at the same time.

"Whoa," yelled Shane, bear-hugging me to keep from falling out of Gordon's arms.

Gordon turned around in a snap and ran like a crazy but strong chicken, dodging huge white boulders as they came tumbling down.

"Go, Gordon, go!" I yelled.

Gordon jumped out of the passageway just as the ceiling caved in.

Ben and Nabila, along with all the monsters, screamed and cheered as Gordon laid Shane and me on the floor.

Even the small failed splurtsar squeed with delight, a bit of black nectar spraying itself all over Gil's scaly butt.

Gordon took a bow and passed out.

"He's going to need quite a nap," said Twenty-Three.

"Twenty-Three!" Shane yelled, standing up. "Dude, you made it!"

"Yes," said Twenty-Three. "And you'll be happy to know that I'm not the only one."

Twenty-Three gestured over to a crowd of monsters, which parted to reveal . . .

"Director Z!" yelled Ben, and he waved with his still-webbed hand.

Director Z waved weakly, and then his head drooped onto his chest. He swayed like a zombie.

"He's still in shock from the last 'treatment' Zorflogg gave him," Twenty-Three said. "But he should be fine. I saw him in the High Security area and led him out when nobody was looking."

"Awesome!" said Shane. "But what'd they do to him?"

"Zorflogg supercharged his—"

Twenty-Three was cut off by screams.

A tall two-legged creature with goat's hooves and the beak of a hawk screeched terribly as it ran up to all of us. It flapped its tentacles with fear.

"Does anyone speak hawkish?" Twenty-Three

asked. "What's wrong, Glebdorf? Calm down and use your words."

"Sector 78!" screeched the bird/squid/goat/human. "Sector 78!"

"Sector 78?" asked Nabila.

"Oh no!" said Twenty-Three, smacking his lizard face with his claw/paw. "I should have known. We're in the supply room of Sector 78. I *knew* this looked familiar."

"Where are the supplies?" I asked. "And what's the big deal about Sector 78?"

A great roar echoed through the cave.

"Sector 78 is the last laboratory Zorflogg ran, but it was overrun by the creatures he created. Zorflog sealed it—and the old lebensplasm mine—off, but we dug so close to it with the new mines that when your friend burped, he reopened it!"

"What sort of creatures are we talking about here?" asked Ben.

"Well, that one, for instance!" said Twenty-Three, pointing at the front of the supply room.

A massive woolly creature lumbered into our cave. Its dirty coat was ragged and in some places bloodied.

"He looks really hungry," I said.

It opened its mouth and roared.

Two more of the massive creatures appeared.

"Wow, this cave felt pretty roomy until those guys got here," said Shane.

I knew we had to attack before they did, or when they charged, they'd scatter us all over the room and would have control.

"Zombies!" I yelled. "Grab Director Z and bring him over next to Gordon. Protect them both!

"Everyone else," I said, "chaaaaaaarge!"

"Gaaaaaaaaaaa!" the monsters from Gallow Manor cried.

The rejected monsters looked confused and scared, but with a quick "c'mon, guys" from Twenty-Three, they fell in line with us. In fact, the first in front of all of us was the small rejected splurtsar.

He ran up to the woolly creatures, and with a great achoo, snorfed a little bit of black nectar into the eyes of one of them. He then jumped up and chomped it with his piggly little mouth, holding on tight.

"ARRRRRGGGGH!"

The others charged. A giant zombie frog with the head of a battering ram jumped into a second woolly creature and knocked him over with a loud OOOOOOF!

The third was suddenly scared and tried to turn around to run.

But it was too late.

The monsters reached the three woolly creatures, and in a flash of fur and flesh, all that was left was a woolly pile of bones and a great circle of blood. Vampires picked meat out of their teeth. Werewolves fought over one of the great creatures' leg bones. Witches collected the wool to determine if it had any magical powers.

We stood in the doorway of the supply room, looking in on a massive, state-of-the-art laboratory built into the moon rock.

"Much of the equipment has been destroyed by the angry creatures that once roamed freely," said Twenty-Three. "Once it was sealed off, the creatures had to fend for themselves."

There was a screeching sound, and huge tentacled heads floated into the laboratory.

Twenty-Three pushed me away from the door.

"Don't let them see you," he hissed. "Or they'll take your brain out through your eye sockets."

Nabila twitched.

"I've seen it before," Twenty-Three continued. "And it's not pretty. Those massive floating heads are the same heads that Andromedans have, but Zorflogg altered them to collect brains instead of lebensplasm."

"How are we going to get past them?" I asked.

"I'm not sure," Twenty-Three replied. "Maybe they're full and won't notice us. Their heads must be filled with dozens of brains—human brains, brains of the new creations, brains of some of the monster and alien guards."

"Did you say brains?!?" Nabila yelled, and ran past us and into the next room. "Aw, YES! I've never been hungrier in my whole entire life."

"Looks like she's still got a little zombie in her, after all," said Shane.

"Nabila!" I yelled. "Stop!"

But there was no stopping Nabila.

There was a scream from the floating brain collectors as she entered the room.

A bloodcurdling scream.

A *hungry* scream.

... And into the Membranium

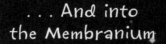

Nabila rushed toward the floating heads and jumped like a possessed wildcat onto the closest tentacled brain collector, ripping into its squishy head with her teeth. She tore a pretty good-size hole for just using her mouth and then dipped her hand in, rummaging around for brains, while the head flew around the room trying to knock her off. The others were closing in to help, gnashing their disgusting teeth that were stained green from all the brains.

"C'mon, we gotta get her before she gets herself killed," I yelled.

"Yahooooo!" yelled Nabila, riding around the room on the brain collector like it was a rodeo bronco. While holding on, she shoved gray matter into her mouth.

I rushed into the room with Ben and Shane, followed by the vampires and Roy.

One of the brain collectors got close enough to get ahold of Nabila with its tentacles. She didn't seem to notice anything but the brains as it pulled itself closer to her and opened its toothy mouth with a hiss.

"Nabila," cried Ben, but she just didn't notice.

The vampires quickly turned into bats and flapped in front of the brain collector that had ahold of Nabila. Perturbed, it loosened its grip a little, and Grigore flitted above the head and turned back into a human, forcing it down to the ground. Roy lumbered over and crushed it.

They did the same with the remaining heads, with more monsters rushing in to help. Soon, knowing that Gordon and Director Z were safe, the other zombies were asked in to feast on the bounty of brains.

Nabila still held on to the first head, which flew higher and higher.

"Nabila, watch out!" I yelled through cupped hands. "It's going to crush you against the moon rock ceiling!"

The brain collector picked up speed, pushing up faster and faster.

CRASH!

Nabila's head hit the ceiling, and her grip started to loosen. The brain collector floated down and then up again—

CRASH!

—hitting the ceiling once again. This time, the impact knocked both of them out, and they came tumbling down toward the ground.

All the vampires were on the ground. Camilla reacted first, quickly turning into a vampire bat and flying up to slow Nabila's fall. As they collided, she transformed back into human form and tumbled toward the ground.

The last of the brain collectors hit the dusty floor first.

Camilla and Nabila landed second in a great pile of what appeared to be dead skin.

"Membranium!" Ben yelled as he rushed over to help.

Camilla, remembering the horrors of Paradise Island, clawed her way out of the pile of skin.

"Get them off me!" she shrieked, her black shoes slipping and squeaking as she made her way to the top of the huge pile.

"What about Nabila?" Ben yelled as Camilla rushed past him into the storage room.

Ben dove into the pile headfirst, with the agility that only a fish could have.

I screamed, "Ben!" and was about to jump into the pile myself when Twenty-Three grabbed my shoulder.

"Don't worry!" yelled Twenty-Three. "Those

membranium are harmless. You have to lead them to their victim and slip them over its head before they wake up enough to cover it. And they're not attached to a host, so they do nothing."

Ben exploded out of the pile of skin, dragging a moaning Nabila with him.

We helped her up, and she was able to sit on a busted old office chair with a huge chunk bitten out. Blood, crusted with moon rock, seeped over her eyes.

"Oh, my head," she said. "It aches so much."

The anteater monster I had seen collecting moondust in the mines came over to me and snorfed at my feet, shaking its hairy little rump back and forth.

"What is it?" I asked.

It pointed its trunk up at Nabila's bleeding head.

"Um," I said, "you want to snorf up her blood?"

It snorfed what I could only assume was "yes" and shook its hairy rump even faster.

"Okay . . . ," I said doubtfully, and picked up the little guy.

I felt its chest expand, and it snorfed up all the blood and moon rock, using its thin little tongue to work out the bigger chunks.

"Ack," Nabila said. "That tickles!"

When it finished, I put it back down again.

"You look great!" I said to Nabila.

"Uggghhhhh," Nabila said.

"Should we get you more brains?" asked Shane, rushing over to one of the zombies that was feasting away on a brain collector.

"Hey!" the zombie protested as Shane swiped a huge wad of gray matter out of its hand, brought it over to Nabila, and shoved it into her mouth.

"Bleeechh," she choked.

"I think that brain collector knocked the last of the zombie out of you," said Shane with a smile.

She barfed all over Ben.

"My, how the tables have turned," said Ben.

Everybody laughed and laughed . . .

. . . until the room began to shake. The beakers and flasks that were left on the shelves tumbled to the ground and shattered.

"Oh no," I said, "what's next?"

A great moan tore through our bodies, shaking our hearts. We held our hands up to our ears to keep them from bleeding.

"That's not any of Zorflogg's creations," said Twenty-Three. "That's the moon. The moon is screaming."

Moon Drain

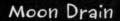

"Everyone grab a membranium!" I yelled over the rumbling and moaning. "Pull it over you!"

The monsters in the supply closet ran into the room as Shane and I passed out membranium to everyone we could as quickly as possible.

A huge boulder shook free from the ceiling and landed on Katherine the witch.

"Noooooo!" Griselda screamed. "My sister!"

All that was left of Katherine was one leg that poked out awkwardly from beneath the boulder. Griselda pulled at the leg as other, smaller stones tumbled from above, knocking her in the head and shoulders.

"Hurry, Griselda!" I yelled. "Or you'll be next!"

Shane grabbed an armful of membranium and passed them to Pietro, who had already put on his.

"Run these to Director Z and Gordon, fast!" Shane yelled over the rumbling.

Huge rocks continued to fall, bouncing off the monsters who had put on the membranium. Those that were too slow didn't stand a chance.

CRUNCH!

The small anteater monster was crushed under a rock.

"Noooooo!" yelled Nabila.

"Hurry, everyone, hurry!" I yelled.

And then, as quickly as it had begun, the moon stopped shaking.

Before we could even breathe sighs of relief, a great screech tore through our ears.

SQUEEEEEEEEEEECH.

"Is that the moon again?" I asked Twenty-Three.

"No, that's the intercom!" said Twenty-Three.

"SUCCESSS!" Zorflogg's voice boomed through speakers hidden all over the room. "The test was a success!" We could hear all his lackeys applauding through the intercom.

"What test?" Shane asked. "Did we pass?"

"I don't think he can hear you," said Twenty-Three.

"The Andromedans have learned how to drain the moon, my scared little children," said Zorflogg over the intercom. "I don't know where you are, and frankly hope the creations I've left scattered around my compound are chewing on your bones as I speak, but just in case, I wanted to make sure tell you about this fantastic news. For this is really all your doing."

His voice broke up for a moment, a shot of static echoing through the room.

"You see, you forced my hand. I wanted to take my time with the moon, to learn how to cultivate 'monster juice,' as you call it. But, in a burst of inspiration, I've moved the process forward. I'll just have to be a little wasteful and drain it all *now*! And why not? It will just make things easier for me on Earth. I've searched your ship, and there is nothing on it. But I will have all eternity and enough lebensplasm to find all the pendants soon. Now you are truly worthless to me. Servants, load up for takeoff! Andromedans, gather above the Apollo Quadrant. My ship will meet you there. Thank you, scared little children, for showing me the way! Wish me a bon voyage, and I wish you a good evening and the quick, painless death of which you are not even worthy."

SCCHHHPPLLUUUURCH!

The intercom cut off. There was silence in Sector 78.

"We've got to destroy that monster before he lets the Andromedans drain the moon!" I said, pacing around nervously. "But how? Wait . . . first things first. Twenty-

Three, how much time do we have?"

"I would think it would take at least twelve hours for Zorflogg to prepare his ship and get into position in the Apollo Quadrant," said Twenty-Three.

"Are you sure?" asked Shane.

"Yes," said Twenty-Three.

"What is the Apollo Quadrant?" I asked. "I've never heard of it."

"It's the area in the moon's orbit that lines up directly with the moon's mouth," replied Twenty-Three. "I think Zorflogg wants to be right above it just in case the moon spits up any raw lebensplasm as it coughs its last breath."

"Whoa, whoa, whoa, wait," said Shane. "So what are we actually talking about here? I just want to be clear."

"Yes, because clarity is your thing . . . ," snickered Nabila. "Ow, my head."

"The moon is a monster, and it has a mouth?" asked Shane excitedly.

"Yes," said Twenty-Three. "The moon is the First Monster, sending its lebensplasm-rich rays down onto the Earth. Monsters soak up the moon like humans soak up the sun."

"How did you not know this?" Shane asked me.

"Have you ever heard of science?" I asked. "I'm pretty sure Mr. Stewart never said anything about the moon being the First Monster."

"Are you sure?" asked Shane. "Because, as you know, I never pay any attention at school."

"Twenty-Three?" Nabila asked. "What did Zorflogg mean when he said that destroying the moon would 'make things easier for me on Earth'?"

"The monsters on Earth will wilt away quickly without the power of the moon. It looks like you've gotten him worried and now he's going to drain the moon completely. Well done!"

"But no moon means no monsters," said Ben. "Oh man."

The monsters started to screech and moan. The zombies began wandering around aimlessly, bumping into walls and weeping. Even Director Z lifted up his head for a moment and moaned.

"Don't give up!" I yelled, and the monsters jumped. "We can't let him destroy the moon!"

I stood up on a half-eaten examination table in front of all the monsters. They turned and looked up at me.

"We will not let the First Monster fail! Somehow, some way, we will prevail over this evil!"

Even Zorflogg's rejected creatures began to gather around me as my speech got louder and more impassioned.

"We're inside a huge source of monster power!" I yelled. "Perhaps the biggest source of monster juice in the known universe! We have twelve hours to figure out how to tap into that power, break out of these caves, and get into space! Let's—"

"Guys, guys!" yelled Gordon from the storage space. "Get in here . . . NOW!"

The monsters growled low growls, and I saw the hair rise up on the backs of the monsters who had hair.

"Oh, man, what's next?" I yelled, and jumped off the table.

We rushed back into the storage space, ready to face another threat.

Master Plan

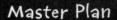

We were ready to attack.

Screaming and growling, we ran into the room ready to strike fear into the heart of whatever disgusting creature had sent Gordon flying to us for help.

Director Z wandered in front of the door, a little drool oozing down his chin, as we charged through. He shrieked with terror.

Gordon's eyes bugged with fear as we rushed to the back of the room.

He held up his hands and waved us off.

"Guys!" he yelled as he stumbled backward. "SHHHHH! Shut up!"

The monsters around us frothed at the mouth and

shook like crazy, ready to tear into whatever happened to make the mistake of walking into the room.

I gave him a strange look.

"Just shut UUUUUP!" he insisted. "Please, Chris, just shut them up!"

"SILENCE," I commanded.

The monsters fell silent.

In the quiet, I could hear the echo of faraway voices.

"What's that?" asked Nabila.

"I think they're guards," said Pietro, his ears twitching slightly.

"Where is it coming from?" asked Ben.

"Look!" Shane said, pointing at a dark corner of the storage room. "A hole in the wall."

There was a human-size hole that must have shaken open when the moon was being tested. Through the hole, I could see the eerie yet familiar glow of the strange globes.

"It's the first tunnel we walked into!" I gasped. "The way back to the ship!"

"That's what I wanted to show you!" said Gordon. "Now keep it down! Or they'll hear us."

"Too late," said Pietro, his hand wrapped around his ear to collect sound better. "They've heard us and are coming to investigate."

"What!" Gordon yelled. "You idiots!"

"Now *you* shut up," I said. "Look—the rocks that fell

out of the wall to make the hole are still sitting in here. Everyone grab a rock and fill in the hole quick. We need to make it look like it was never here. Hurry!"

Monsters large and small rushed up to grab whatever size rock they could to fill in the hole.

"Hurry," I said.

"We need to get some of the bigger rocks in there," Shane said.

Frederick, who was good and charged up from the zapping that the werewolves had done to him, grabbed a big boulder and slammed it into place.

But it wasn't quite enough.

The voices in the tunnel got louder as Roy stomped up and grabbed the largest boulder. He lifted it over his head, ready to slam it home.

"Wait!" Ben whispered. "Gently!"

Roy gritted his teeth and slowly, achingly set the boulder into place with the faintest *sssscccccccccrch*.

We all stayed very, very quiet. Even the wildest of the monsters knew that they should keep it down.

The concerned voices passed the newly filled hole, and Pietro shoved his ear up against the pile of rocks.

"They've moved on," he said.

"Are you okay?" Shane asked Gordon.

"Zorflogg woke me up with his crazy message," said Gordon. "I've just been sort of resting since then. Until I heard the guards and crawled over to see where it was coming from, only to see the globes."

"That means we have access to the ship," I yelled, excited.

"SHHH!" scolded Pietro. "They're still close."

"I never got to thank you," I whispered to Gordon. "You saved me."

"You saved me, too!" whispered Shane, and he gave Gordon a very slow high five.

"You saved *all* of us," said Nabila. "You were amazing."

"Yeah, man!" said Ben. "How do you feel? That sounded like the most relieving burp in the history of man. I'm totally jealous."

"I feel good," said Gordon. "Exhausted but good."

"I know what you mean," I said. "I'm beat. This is the first time we've stopped running since we landed on the moon."

I slumped down on a moon boulder.

"Me too!" said Shane and Nabila at the same time.

"I could really use a drink of blood . . . um, I mean, a nap," said Shane. He checked his teeth with his tongue one more time. "Nope . . . all gone."

"I feel pretty good," said Ben, flexing his webbed hands a little. "Swampy and fit."

"I could have napped for a few more years," said Gordon. "But something hit me in the head. A boulder, now that I think of it . . . like, as big as the one under your butt, Chris. But why wasn't my head crushed?"

"You're wearing a membranium," Shane said. "Pietro slipped it over your head while you were sleeping."

"We're all wearing them," I said.

"Ugh, that kinda freaks me out," said Gordon. He turned green and hugged himself.

"It's okay," I said. "Twenty-Three said they're not attached to a host. In fact, it's good! We have a little extra protection, and I'm guessing we're going to need it."

"How can we be sure?" asked Gordon. "I'm going to feel itchy. We better not have to wear them for too long. Maybe I can burp again and blow it off. I don't have time for all that fartin'."

"Be careful it doesn't get blown back in your face," said Nabila. "That was one incredibly powerful burp."

"Blown back . . . ," Gordon said, thinking.

"What is it?" Shane asked.

"I think I've got an idea!" yelled Gordon.

Nabila started to *shush* him, but Pietro said, "It's okay, they're gone."

"What is it?" I asked.

"Are there more membranium?" Gordon asked.

"There's a large tank deeper in the laboratory, right before you get to the old refining machine. There might be some more in there," said Twenty-Three. "Why?"

"We need to stuff the Andromedans inside the membranium!" Gordon yelled, pacing around and slamming his fist into his hand. "Yes! Wrap them up tight. Then, when they start vurping . . ."

"Their vurp would expand the membranium," added Shane. "Even if they were in space."

"And then when they burped their thunderburp—" said Nabila.

"They'd blow themselves up," I finished.

"I mean, you saw what happened when I burped," said Gordon. "The epic sound waves destroyed them all. So, what if we could find enough membranium to toss on every last Andromedan?"

"There's no guarantee there are any in the tank," said Twenty-Three. "But you never know!"

"We've got to give it a try," I said.

As if to back up my statement, another sad, low moan came from the moon. The room shook slightly.

"I think he agrees," Gordon said.

"What makes you think the moon is a 'he'?" asked Nabila.

"Fine," said Gordon. "She agrees. Or it agrees."

"I think our best bet is 'it,'" said Shane.

"We just have to hope that there are enough membranium in there," Gordon said.

"And that we don't get eaten alive . . . ," added Shane.

"What do you mean 'we'?" asked Ben, pointing to his gills. "I think this is more of a 'me' thing. A swamp thing."

"You're still fully powered up?" I asked.

"As far as I can tell," Ben said.

He lifted up his shirt and slapped his strong, scaly abs.

WHORF!

With a splatter, a little green ooze spewed out of his mouth.

"Strange," he said. "That felt good . . ."

"Great," I said. "We've got a ship, even if it's half-busted. We've learned how to create monster juice from moon rock, and there's another refinery on the other side of the lab. We just need to grab the membranium, power up the monsters, and get on board."

"So what do we do about the half-busted ship?" said Nabila. "If we pull away from the cave, all the air will get sucked out of the huge tear."

"Frederick," I said, "do you know how to repair it?"

"Sorry, Boss," he said. "When I'm in the system, I can tell what's going on with the ship, but I can't do much more than turn things on and off."

"Can you seal off the cargo hold?" I asked.

"I can close the doors, yes," he said.

"But then how would we fit everyone on the ship?" asked Ben.

Director Z wandered back over to us again. His head was down, and he was snoring.

"I bet you he would know," I said. "Once we get the

monster juice flowing, we should give him a drink and see if it snaps him out of this. He knew about the ship before we did. Maybe he knows how to repair it."

"There's no need to wait," said Shane, pulling a small glass bottle out of his pocket. "Nabila and I didn't drink all of ours!"

He pulled out the bottle and handed it to me.

"Is it enough?" I asked, staring at it.

"There's only one way to find out," said Gordon, who stopped Director Z as he wandered past in his endless circle. Gordon tilted Director Z's head back, and the Director snored loudly.

SNNNNNNNNNAAAARRRRRCHHHH!

Gordon propped his mouth open for me . . .

SNNNNNNNNNAAAAA—

. . . and pinched his nose. I let the oozy monster juice drip into his mouth.

GULP.

Director Z snapped to attention, eyes blazing red, and pulled himself swiftly out of Gordon's grasp.

"I will destroy ALL you!" Director Z yelled.

He grabbed me by the neck, and fangs sprang out of his bloody mouth.

I saw stars as he tightened his grip.

Moon Madness

"Director Z!" yelled Shane. "Let him go!"

"Director Z!" Gordon yelled. "Director Z! Listen!"

Gordon jumped up and grabbed Director Z's hands, but they didn't even budge.

I could feel myself passing out, and saw the monsters rushing toward Director Z as the light faded from my eyes.

His grip released and I hit the floor, and Director Z yelled, "WAIT!"

I looked up to see Director Z shaking as he struggled to control his monstrous powers.

But the monsters closed in. They would not listen to him.

The vampires hissed at Director Z, disgusted by his violent outburst. The werewolves growled a low growl. Even the smaller creatures rushed forward. A small zombie squirrel chattered its teeth. Roy picked up Director Z even easier than he had picked up the rock before, and held him above his head. My mind was still woozy from lack of oxygen, my body was beyond exhausted, but before Roy could slam Director Z against the rocks . . .

"WAIT!" I yelled.

This time the monsters listened.

"Put him down," I said to Roy.

Roy threw him onto the floor.

"OOF."

"You forgot to say 'gently,'" said Shane.

We ran over to Director Z and helped him up, hoping he was himself again.

"Are you okay?" I asked him.

"I think so," he said, licking his new vampire teeth. "Are you okay?"

"I think so," I said.

"You gave me monster juice?" he asked. "That must be the reason for my sudden anger. My apologies. It was the first time in hours that I had any thought in my head, and the thought was an overwhelming one: 'kill.' I have to say, I have a newfound respect for the residents now that I've felt the powerful emotions they experience."

A few of the monsters around us nodded, agreeing with him.

"How did you know that I hadn't drunk monster juice before?" Director Z asked me. "You do realize what would have happened if I had."

"We didn't really think it through," I said. "We just did it. We really need your help."

I updated Director Z on everything that had happened since Zorflogg took him away. A few of the monsters added details here and there.

"So, you see," I finished, "we need to figure out how to repair the ship, power up the monsters, and lead them to battle with the membranium in hand. And then there's the question of how to defeat Zorflogg. I haven't even begun to figure that out. My brain hurts. I'm totally tired. Totally burned out. I'm so glad you're back."

"As am I," replied Director Z. "However, I can help you in very limited ways. As you saw from before, the monsters won't take orders from me anymore. They would have killed me if you hadn't stopped them. I have no pendant. And I'm *very* proud that you've held on to yours. Well done. Not even I had thought of hiding it there."

"That reminds me," said Shane. "I've been meaning to ask where—"

Before he could ask where, Director Z continued, "It is you who must lead them into battle, Chris."

"But you still know so much," I said, trying hard not to whine. "You have to teach me what you know. And what about the ship?"

"I will guide you as I can," Director Z replied. "And as for the ship, I'll explain to Frederick the way he can focus his power to melt the crack back together. Once the residents have drunk the moon's fresh, rich monster juice, we can get on board, make the repair as quickly as possible, and head into orbit. And I think that your idea of using the membranium is a good one, Gordon. I think it will work. But you are correct—we still must figure out how to defeat Zorflogg in his well-shielded ship. He is a relentless creature. He will stop at nothing now that he's set his mind to destroying the moon."

"Tell me more about Zorflogg," I said. "You knew him? Why does he hate the old monsters so much?"

"He doesn't believe in the Code of Monsterdom, for one," replied Director Z.

"What's the Code of Monsterdom?" asked Nabila.

"It lays out all of the rules that monsters must obey in a world of humans," said Director Z. "I won't get into details—in fact, I mustn't, or I'd have to kill you—but the part of the Code that Zorflogg finds so terrible is the rule that says monsters are only allowed to scare humans, not harm them. They are required to maintain a balance with the human race."

"I take it he'd rather just eat us?" asked Shane.

"It's more complicated than that," replied Director Z. "The Code was laid down to protect humans, but Zorflogg believes that the monster race should rule the Earth. He aims, with the help of his new breed, to take over the world. Any old monsters that don't fall into place shall be crushed along with the human race. He believes that by not rising up with him, the old monsters proved they, too, must be destroyed."

"So we'll destroy him first!" yelled Gordon.

"Yeah," yelled Twenty-Three, his lizard fist in the air.

"It remains to be seen if that is possible," said Director Z. "However, I think that Zorflogg has made one mistake that might help us."

"What's that?" I asked.

"He's turned his back on the moon," said Director Z. "Zorflogg is right to think that the moon—the First Monster—holds the key to all power in monsterdom. But what Zorflogg has forgotten because he is so drunk on power is that the moon is itself an incredibly powerful monster that can give power to other monsters."

"So we're not the only ones who are given power by the moon?" asked Howie.

"Yes and no," said Director Z. "Werewolves have always had a special relationship with the moon—a closer bond. Have you ever noticed how, of all the monsters in the retirement home, it was they who had the most power when you first arrived, Chris?"

"Yes," I said. "Pietro was always winning all the bingo games."

"I knew there vas a reason!" yelled Grigore, and he shook his fist at Pietro.

All our monsters began to protest, and Director Z held up his hand to silence them.

But everyone kept yelling at Pietro.

Director Z gave me a look.

"Oh right," I said.

I held up my hand to silence them.

They obeyed.

"Yes, the werewolves were more powerful," continued Director Z. "Because they spent more time with the moon. They ran in moonlight, no matter how tired they were. They had conversations with the moon. But all monsters are influenced by the moon's power. And the moon can choose which monsters to give the most power to."

"Wait," said Shane. "The moon talks back?"

"I always thought I was just hearing voices," said Howie.

"Knowing you," Gordon said, "you might just be hearing voices."

"So how can we use the moon to our benefit?" I asked.

"That is another great mystery," said Director Z.

"The moon usually keeps to itself. But you've already been helped along—more than once—and I'm sure the moon is very much interested in aiding in our success. If we win, the moon rises again. I'm sure we'll be rewarded greatly."

"And if we don't win," said Nabila, "not only are we dead, but the entire world as we know it is gone. POOF!"

"Oh man," I said, clutching my stomach. "It's sickening."

"I agree," said Shane. "Thinking of the end of the world will definitely give you indigestion. Or garlic. Garlic and I don't get along."

"You're tellin' me," said Vlad.

"No, that's not it," I whispered to Shane. "I have to . . ."

"Have to . . . ," Shane said.

"Number two," I whispered.

"What's the big deal?" Shane asked. "I think there was a bathroom in the laboratory."

"Because . . . ," I whispered even more quietly.

"What?" Shane asked, leaning in.

"I ate the pendant," I whispered. "That's how I hid it. And I don't want the monsters to know, because what if it freaks them out that I pooped all over their pendant?"

"I see," said Shane. "Can I help?"

"No," I said. "I'm pretty sure I need to do this alone.

But I really appreciate that you asked, despite the fact that it's totally weird. I'm just not looking forward to eating it again."

"Did you know some nomads eat their own poop?" Shane asked. "To battle dysentery."

"No way!" I yelled. "How do you know these crazy facts?"

"Go on, then, nomad," said Shane. "Do your thing."

I slowly limped away, trying not to go in my pants.

"The rest of you get a little sleep," said Director Z. "It'll be the last bit of rest that you'll get before—"

"The monster space battle to end all monster space battles?" Gordon asked.

"I wouldn't say it exactly that way," said Director Z. "But yes."

"Yeah, guys," I yelled over my shoulder, "you heard Director Z. Take a nap. I've got some important business to take care of."

Director Z gave me a thumbs-up as I headed for the bathroom.

Take the Plunge

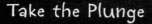

It took me so long to do my duty, clean off the pendant, and—after several failed attempts—force it down again that by the time I got back to everyone else, I had no time for napping. I just had to push forward. My body ached from lack of sleep and the thought of what was floating around inside me.

"How was it?" Shane asked, stretching after his catnap.

"Not so bad," I said. "But it made me realize how hungry I was. The only thing I've had since we left Earth was the pendant—twice—and little bits and pieces of Andromedans."

"Don't forget the monster juice," said Shane. "That

stuff has to be packed with essential vitamins and minerals."

Pietro had his hairy ear pressed up against the wall.

"I hear lots of growling and yelling," he said, listening hard. "Something about Sector 66."

"Sector 66 is where everyone loads into Zorflogg's ship," Twenty-Three said. "Ah, how long I've dreamed of that day."

"No time for dreaming, Twenty-Three," I said. "We have a lot to take care of, and it makes me nervous that Zorflogg's ship is already being loaded."

"First stop: creepy moon laboratory!" yelled Shane.

Twenty-Three guided me, Ben, Nabila, Shane, and Gordon into the laboratory along with half of the monsters. Director Z and the other half of the monsters stood watch near the filled-in hole in the wall, just in case someone (or something) broke through.

We passed by the rotting carcasses of the brain-eating Andromedan mutations.

"Would you care for any leftovers?" Shane asked Nabila.

"Please don't joke," she said, vurping a few brains into her mouth. "Ugh, they taste even worse on the way up."

"At least you're full," I said.

As we went deeper into the laboratory, whole chunks of ceiling and wall had crumbled all over the floor,

The lights that weren't completely shattered flickered ominously. We walked past cages that smelled even worse than the brain-eating Andromedan carcasses.

"I wonder what was in there," said Ben.

"Whatever it was, I hope it's gone for good," said Nabila.

I looked nervously into each dark corner as we approached. The hair on the back of Howie's neck raised as he turned into dog form, knocking a tray off an experiment table. Wendy the banshee screeched.

"Well, if anyone's down here, they'll know where to find us," I said.

"Sorry," said Wendy.

We all paused.

Listening . . .

Waiting . . .

All we could hear were the huffs and puffs of the older monsters.

The small rejected splurtsar nervously nudged Gordon's pant leg.

"Wha!" he yelled, surprised. "Back off, bacon! Haven't you ever heard of personal space?"

The little splurtsar SQUUUEEED around the corner.

"Sounds like he's okay," said Twenty-Three, and he kept walking. "We're good!"

We turned the last corner, and saw a towering glass

tank, crusted with dark green, slimy algae.

"How are you going to see in there?" Nabila asked Ben. She held his webbed hand tightly.

"I'm not sure," Ben said. He craned his neck to look all the way up to the opening of the tank at the top, near the ceiling of the massive cave. "I don't even know how to get into it."

We walked up to the tank. The closer we got, the more it smelled like sewage.

Ben took a deep breath. "Oh man," he said. "That smells great!"

"My brother!" yelled Gil, walking over to Ben. "I knew that you were one of my kind. I could see it in you. The way your body couldn't control the spew that came out of it. You barf like a swamp creature!"

"Swamp creatures barf?" asked Ben. "I thought you guys all had swamp gas."

"Yes," he said, "I was gifted with the beauteous swamp gas. Some of the strongest of my kind. But there is also swamp muck . . ."

"Diarrhea," said Shane. "Right?"

"The swamp chunks . . . ," said Gil.

"Barf, right?" asked Shane.

"And the swamp nuggets . . . ," said Gil.

"Boogers?" asked Gordon.

"No," said Gil. "I'm referring to those beautiful sticky chunks that get stuck between my webbed toes."

"Oh, toe jam!" I said.

"I like to call it 'fin jam,'" said Gil. "Our kind is so used to the wet world, lots of fungi and other things grow all around us. And liquid or gas always spews from deep in our bodies. I knew the way you spewed, you were one of us!"

He gave Ben such a huge hug that a juicy little fart escaped from both of them.

"Whoa," said Ben. "That felt weird."

A growl from deep inside the tank broke the awkward silence.

"Be careful," I said. "We have no idea what's in there. Or do we, Twenty-Three?"

"No, not for sure," said Twenty-Three. "But I think the only underwater creatures that were ever created by Zorflogg were the membranium. Maybe different types of those? Any membranium without power, like the ones we need, would be deep in the bottom of the tank. Be wary of any membranium that you see floating near the surface."

"Got it," said Ben. "I'm ready."

Gil grabbed Ben by the finned hand and squeezed tight.

"I will explore this disgusting tank with you!" he exclaimed. "I will not fail you, my brother!"

"Are you sure?" asked Ben. "I think that I'd be better off alone. I can handle whatever's down there."

Something slimy and black scraped against the glass in a flash. A deep roar rattled our teeth.

"Where's the Kraken when you need him?" asked Shane.

"On second thought," said Ben, "it might be good to have some company."

"Great!" yelled Gil, and jumped onto the glass wall of the tank using his hands as suction cups.

"Wait!" Ben said. "We can do that? Awesome!"

Ben quickly took his clothes off and jumped up on the glass with Gil. His scales covered up any sensitive areas, but Nabila still blushed.

SCHLUP SCHLUP SCHLUP.

Ben and Gil slowly made their way up to the top of the tank and jumped in with a SPLASH.

Then it was deathly silent.

We stood and watched, waiting for something to happen.

"I feel like it's been twenty minutes," said Gordon.

"One minute and twenty-three seconds," said Twenty-Three.

CRUNCH CRUNCH CRUNCH.

"What's that?" asked Shane.

Nabila and I rushed up to the tank.

CRUNCH CRUNCH CRUNCH.

"Are they being eaten alive?" asked Nabila.

"Sorry, it's just me," said Jill the zombie.

She nervously nibbled her nails.

CRUNCH CRUN—

"Stop it!" I yelled. "You're hitting bone!"

Nabila turned to the tank.

"I wish I could see what's going on in there," she said.

"I wish I could hear what's going on in there," I said.

"I hear you!" said Ben.

There was a cheer behind me, and ahead of me through the muck, I could barely make out Ben.

"How are you able to speak?" I yelled.

"Fartspeak," he fartsaid, a few bubbles rising from his scaly swamp-creature butt. "Found membranium!"

He pointed at Gil, who we could barely make out collecting dozens and dozens of membranium at the bottom of the tank.

Suddenly, there was a flash. Then a second. Then a third. It was so intense, it hurt my eyes, even through the algae.

"An electric eel," I yelled, pointing behind Ben. "It's huge!"

The eel flashed once more and knocked Gil over with its gnarled tail.

"I forgot about the eels," said Twenty-Three.

"Did you say 'eels'?" I asked. "As in 'more than one'?"

"Well, on the bright side, at least they'll be able to see what's going on in there," said Shane.

"If that's the bright side of what's going on in there," said Nabila, "I'm a little worried about what the dark side is."

Ben pushed off the glass and swam over to Gil, picking him up quickly. Nabila pressed her face against the glass to get a better look, but another eel came out of nowhere and zapped the algae, cooking it against the glass.

"I can't see what's happening," she yelled.

"We're okay," fartyelled Ben.

But it looked like a thunderstorm was trapped in the tank. The eels zapped constantly. The water began to bubble at the top of the tank.

"Hurry, Gil!" Ben fartscreamed.

There was another huge flash, and then . . .

"Arrrrgh!" Ben fartscreamed so loudly it rattled the glass and our ears.

"Ben!" screamed Nabila.

A huge net, filled with membranium, flew out of the top of the tank—a huge, wet ball. It hit the ceiling and flew down to the floor, bouncing once, twice, and coming to a stop against the far wall.

Gil exploded out of the tank and grabbed onto the ceiling.

"Waaaaagh!" he yelled.

An eel splashed up and out of the tank after him, headed right for his frazzled old swamp-creature butt, mouth open wide, razor-sharp black teeth exposed.

FLLLLLUUUUUUUURRRRRRRPT!

Gil farted directly into the gaping mouth of the eel. Dazed, it crashed into the ceiling, and then flopped back into the tank.

"Oh man, that's epic!" yelled Shane. "Yeah, Gil!"

Gil fell from the ceiling onto the lip of the tank, quickly SCHLUP SCLUPPING down the side.

"Where's Ben?" screamed Nabila, rushing over to Gil. "Where is he? Is he safe?"

"I tried so hard," said Gil. "But he's not a swamp creature anymore."

"What does that mean?" Nabila yelled. "Go back in there and get him!"

"I was too late," Gil said, and he put a webbed hand over his face and began to weep.

Barfball

Nabila began to cry. Shane walked over and hugged her. Some of the monsters started to sniffle and wail.

I stomped over to Gil, holding back tears. I needed answers.

"Too late?" I asked, grabbing him by the shoulders. "What does that mean?"

"I failed him," he said. "He'll never be a swamp creature again. I took away his gift."

"How?" I asked. "He had a membranium on."

"His fartspeaking filled it up slightly," said Gil, green ooze coming out of his nose. "One zap from the eel was all it took to weaken the skin. A second drained him of—"

BAAAARRRRRRRF.

"What was that?" asked Nabila. "That is the exact sound Ben makes when he's sick!"

She rushed up to the tank one more time and screamed, "BENNNN!"

"Ugh, I'm choking," a weak voice came from somewhere.

"Look," Gordon yelled, pointing at the net of membranium. Barf oozed out of the sides.

WHAAARRRRRF.

More chunks spilled out of the tightly wound ball of membranium. It splashed out of the sides like a geyser.

"Get. Me. Out," Ben said.

Camilla quickly turned into a vampire bat and used her extremely sharp teeth to cut into the netting. All at once, the netting broke, sending barf-soaked membranium spilling out onto the moon-rock floor. With it came . . .

"Ben!" yelled Nabila. We all ran over to him, slipping on the membranium.

"I'm okay," he said. "Just sick."

"And naked," I said, covering his butt with a barf-stained membranium.

"So everything is normal again," said Shane. "None of us are monsters."

"Like I said," Gil said, walking over with Ben's clothes, still sniffling, "Ben has lost his powers. I'm so sorry, my brother. When the last eel zapped the swamp creature out of you, I threw you into the middle of the membranium and tied up the net. I figured you'd be safe in there."

"It was a bit rough coming out of the tank," said Ben. "How many times did I bounce? It felt like seven hundred."

I shielded him while he got dressed.

"No wonder you were sick, *habibi*," said Nabila, gently stroking his wet hair. She pulled chunks of goo out of his ears.

"He's sick because I let those terrible creatures drain his powers," wailed Gil.

"No, he's sick because he's Ben," I said, lifting him up and patting him on the back.

"You saved me, Gil," Ben said. "Thank you. I couldn't have stayed a swamp creature forever, anyway. That wouldn't have worked out so well at school."

"What happened with the membranium?" I asked Ben. "Gil said your bit of fartspeaking weakened it."

"It might have been because it was stretched," Ben said. "But I think it was actually because of the eel's electric shock."

"Yeah, it must be weakened by electricity," Gordon said. "Look at what Gil was able to do—fart that gnarly fart right through it!"

"I don't think we'll be dealing with any electricity

in space," I said. "But I don't think we can trust the membranium we have on to protect us. And how can we be sure that the membranium won't just pop when the Andromedans thunderburp?"

Before anyone could answer, Director Z came rushing into the room.

"Chris," he said, panting. "Pietro's telling us that he can't hear anything but the rumble of an engine."

All of Zorflogg's rejected creations began to chatter nervously.

"The engines start warming up about thirty minutes before takeoff," Twenty-Three said.

"But we don't even know how we're going to deal with Zorflogg's ship when we get up there!" I said, already feeling defeated. "And we've still got to refine enough monster juice to power everyone up."

"With all those eels blasting electricity around the tank, I got an idea," said Ben. "I mean, an idea about how to deal with Zorflogg's ship."

"What is it?" I asked.

"Remember those globes plugged into the moon?" Ben asked.

"You mean, the glowy ones?" asked Shane.

"Yes," said Ben. "Those. They're tapped into the power of the moon somehow. What if we did the same thing and ran a cable from the moon to our ship?"

"That would have to be a really long cable," I said,

turning to Twenty-Three. "Is there something like that on the moon?"

"There might be some extra cable in the old refinery," replied Twenty-Three. "It's just up ahead, in the next set of caves."

"Well, let's get going," I said. "We've got an insane amount of work to do to mine monster juice in preparation for takeoff. Director Z, please come with me back to the supply room. I'll grab the rest of the monsters and guide them back to the refinery. You get on the ship and get it ready. I know for sure that it needs some repairs."

"I'll do what I can," he said.

"Everyone else, get to mining," I said. "Twenty-Three, do you think you can turn on the refiner?"

"I'll try my best," he replied. "Some of the other creatures that worked in the other mine got a peek at the old refiner before it was off-limits. They might have some insight."

"Great!" I said.

Director Z and I jogged back through the laboratory to the supply room.

"Chris, wait just one minute," said Director Z.

"What is it?" I asked as we stopped in front of the terribly smelly cages.

"I just wanted to say that you're doing great," said Director Z. "Really, I mean it. You remind me of myself . . . in my younger days."

"Thanks, Director Z," I replied. "That means a lot."

"Just remember one thing," he said.

"What's that?" I asked.

"Sometimes, to be a Director of monsters, you need to be monstrous," he said, flashing his vampire teeth. "Don't hesitate to show them who's boss."

I paused for a second, thinking about his advice . . .

. . . and then we ran for our lives.

Things Just
Got Crazy

Thirty minutes later, everyone who could hold a pickax was still slamming one into rock. The room was hazy with moondust. Monsters grunted and gasped. Zorflogg's former slaves ran around, desperately trying to feed the crusher. Twenty-Three was on the other end, watching what was coming out.

"Earthlings," said Twenty-Three. "This isn't good."

"What do you mean?" I asked, throwing down my pickax.

I almost tripped over a cat-size slug pulling along a wheelbarrow as I approached Twenty-Three. The refining machine sputtered and shook, tickling my toes inside my shoes when I approached. My teeth felt jittery.

GRRRRRIIIIIINNNNNNNNDDDD!

"It's only one small flask worth of lebensplasm," said Twenty-Three. "There was probably a reason Zorflogg abandoned this machine. The combination crusher-refiner never quite worked."

"That's nowhere near enough!" I yelled. "The monsters are already weakened from all of the mining."

"The good news," said Twenty-Three, "is that we were able to find more than enough cable to connect the moon to your ship." He pointed to a huge pile of coiled-up metal cable behind the refiner. "I kind of figured we would, since everything around here is powered by the moon's energy."

"In other good news," said Shane, "you're soon going to be able to visit Earth, Twenty-Three!"

"If. We. Survive," Nabila said. "Why do you guys always forget?"

"I think it's because Shane has the happy gene, just like Twenty-Three," I said. "C'mon, I need everyone to get serious."

Suddenly, my feet felt like they were going to fly out from under me, the ground shook so hard. My teeth went from jittery to jackhammery.

"Zorflogg's ship must be taking off," said Twenty-Three, holding on to the machine.

"Well, I'm not so happy anymore," said Shane. "I'm ready to get serious."

The shaking slowed and stopped. The refiner stopped with it, choking on the last bits of moon rock.

RRRUUUUUNNNNCCHHHSPPPPLLLLRRRFT!

"Well, we don't need that piece of junk anymore anyway," Gordon said, kicking its metal legs. "OW!"

"But we need your foot!" I yelled. "Everyone, focus! We've got to get into the ship as soon as possible. Gordon, Shane, Roy, and Grigore, grab the cable and run it to the ship. Twenty-Three, hold on to that bottle tight. It's not much, but we'll ration it out to the weaker monsters. Everybody, go, GO, GOOO—"

PPPPPPPSSSHHHHHHHHHHTTTTT!

A huge geyser erupted in the middle of the cave, spewing gooey, creamy, green slime everywhere.

"Pure, unrefined lebensplasm!" Twenty-Three screamed.

The monsters stood, frozen in place, as the geyser stopped, and the last of the monster juice splashed down onto the ground with a SPPPPPPLLLLLUUUURT!

"The moon . . . ," said Shane.

". . . is helping us," I finished.

A small pond had formed in the middle of the cave.

Before I could tell the monsters what to do, they all ran up to the edge and jumped in.

"Wahoooo!" yelled Pietro, and he dove in headfirst.

"Don't drink it all!" yelled Jill.

All the monsters laughed and howled with glee.

"First come, first served," yelled Frederick, and he belly flopped in, splashing the goop all around.

A bit splattered on Nabila's arm.

SIZZZLLLE.

"It burns!" she yelled. "Get it off!"

"I guess Director Z was right," said Ben, rushing over to her. "We can't ever touch this stuff again."

Before Ben could get there, Twenty-Three crawled up Nabila's leg lapped up the monster juice on her arm. His eyes turned red immediately, and he hissed. He opened up the small flask of monster juice he was carrying, pulled out the cork, and GULP GULP GULP!

He screeched and dug his lizardy claws into Nabila.

"Twenty-Three, that hurts," she yelled.

"Feels. GOOD. To. MEEEE," he moaned.

"GET HIM OFF ME," she yelled.

Gordon rushed up and pulled Twenty-Three off Nabila. He flung him onto the ground, but before he hit, wings burst out of his back, and he took off for the pond.

He dove into the muck with the rest of the monsters, who were completely submerged. Random hands popped out of the surface. An occasional bubble popped, sending a roar echoing through the huge cave.

"Something tells me this isn't going to be good," said Gordon, backing away from the pond.

The monster juice bubbled and frothed, and slowly lowered, revealing heads with angry red eyes.

SLLLLUUUUUURRRP.

"Guys, get out of here!" I yelled to my friends. "I'm not sure I'll be able to control them."

SLLLLLUUUUUURRRROOOOOOOOAAARRR!

The monsters emptied the pond and began frantically licking the sticky monster juice off one another.

"I barely recognize them," Shane said. "Look at Grigore."

Grigore's fingers were long and bony, with terrifyingly sharp fingernails at the tips. He opened up his mouth with a great, satisfied roar. Every single tooth was a fang. He flexed his powerful arms, and the popping of his joints echoed throughout the cave.

The monsters stumbled up out of the sticky hole in the ground, their arms outstretched.

"Go!" I yelled to my friends. "Get to the ship! Tell Director Z to get ready. Grab the cable and run it through the tear."

ROOOOOOAAAAAR!

The cable began to unspool as my friends ran. The crazed monsters followed.

"STOP!" I commanded so loudly that the cave shook, small rocks shaking out of the ceiling and raining down on us.

The monsters all turned slowly to me, their bodies heaving as they huffed and puffed. They were strong.

They were insane with monster power. They were the most terrifying monsters I'd ever seen.

Jaws snapped. Frederick was so powered up, he sent a shower of sparks into the air.

All at once, they rushed at me.

"How dare you disobey your Director?" I yelled, holding up my hands. "Or have you forgotten that I hold the pendant of power?"

Some stopped, whimpering as they realized what they had almost done. Just as many kept rushing toward me, the zombies stumbling forward in the lead, their arms pinwheeling like crazy.

Remembering what Director Z had told me, I let the zombies come at me . . .

. . . and ripped off John's arm.

The other monsters stopped, stunned.

I held his arm high and said, "You will listen to me, or you will be punished!" John's finger pointed at them.

"I am your Director, and you *will* do what I say. I am not your enemy. I am your friend. My friends are your friends. The Andromedans are the enemy. You will listen to me. You will listen to my friends. You will listen to Director Z. And we will crush the Andromedans!"

A great roar went up in the cave.

"To the ship!" I yelled, pointing with John's arm. "Let's show the Andromedans the real terror that awaits on the dark side of the moon!"

Takeoff!

By the time we reached the tunnel with the glowing globes, the moon rock was shaking violently around us.

The moon was in trouble.

As soon as the last of us crawled up into the ship, Director Z turned Frederick back around so he was facing the huge metallic tear in the cargo hold.

"Remember what I taught you!" he commanded. "Seal it up!"

Frederick looked at me doubtfully.

"You heard me down there," I said. "You are to obey my friends and Director Z."

Frederick reached out his long, strong arms and grabbed either side of the tear.

"ARRRRRGHHHHHHH!"

He pumped his energy into the metal, heating it so he could bend it back into place.

As the tear closed, we could see the passageway the moon had opened up earlier crumble away with a great crash. The vacuum of space rushed in, sucking all the air through the crack.

Frederick was being pulled into the crack. The werewolves rushed up and bit into his pants to pull him back.

"Hurry!" I yelled. "Seal it up, Frederick."

"WAAAARRRRGH!"

He pulled the crack tight and, with a great electric shock, melted the two sides into place.

ZAAAAAAAP!

"Get to the engine room," Director Z said to him.

Frederick looked at me once again.

"Do it!" I said.

The ship shook violently.

"The Andromedans must already be attacking the moon," said Nabila. "We've got to hurry."

"I'm sure some of them will be drawn to the ship when we take off," I said. "And we'll battle them in space, above the moon. Everyone gear up!" I tossed John his arm. "Those who don't need to breathe will still need jetpacks. Don't forget to grab a membranium!"

Everyone rushed to the supply closets.

"I must stay on the ship," Director Z said. "If the monsters don't obey me in the heat of battle, it could be devastating. You saw what happened with Frederick, but I think he understands now. Plus, I can pilot the ship and figure out with Frederick how to work with whatever energy the moon provides us through the cable. If we can focus it up to the front of the ship, we might be able to send a concentrated blast forward."

"Let me know when we're close enough to the Andromedans," I said. "Then I'll have Frederick blow us out of the cargo hold."

"I'll make sure the door is pointed right at the Andromedans," said Director Z.

He rushed up to the bridge. The ship began to hum and whirr. Frederick must have sat down in the electric chair.

I rushed over to my friends, who were almost completely suited up in the leathery space suits that we found on board. Ben locked his glass helmet into place with a PPPPSSSSSSSSHT.

"These are actually pretty comfortable," Nabila said. "But I hope that crazy old scientist knew what he was doing. Something tells me he didn't have any time to test this stuff out. And I'm sure he had no idea about the Andromedans."

"Let's hope the membranium do what they're supposed to do," said Gordon. "The ones on us and the ones we'll be putting on them."

"I'm thinking if we get them on the Andromedans right before they thunderburp, they should hold," I said. Then I turned to the crowd of monsters. "Did you hear that? Wait until the last minute to slip the membranium over the Andromedans."

They all growled in agreement, from the smallest of Zorflogg's creations to the tallest banshee.

The ship lurched forward suddenly and rose above the moon.

"Helmets on, everyone!" I yelled. "Here we go!"

With the reduced g-forces and lack of atmosphere, it wasn't long before we were up in the moon's orbit, floating around the air lock.

The monsters chattered nervously. I turned to my friends.

"Guys," I said, "be careful out there. Let the monsters do most of the work. Try to stay away from the battle. Just move them around where they're needed. They're so much stronger than us."

Twenty-Three flapped over to Nabila, drooling slightly.

"Get that freak away from me," she screeched.

"We've all got to work together," I said. "That goes for both of you."

"Tasty," said Twenty-Three.

"Gross," said Nabila. "Kill Andromedans! Kill any

Andromedans that are far from me."

"Yes, Tasty," said Twenty-Three. "For you I will do."

"We're all set, Chris!" yelled Director Z over the intercom. "I've got them in my sights."

"Is everyone ready?" I asked through my helmet radio. I tucked a few membranium under the belt of my space suit.

"ROOOOOOAAAR!" said the monsters. My head ached from the noise.

"All monsters, please mute your helmets," I commanded.

"Ready," said Nabila.

"Let's do this," said Shane.

"I wish I were still a swamp creature," said Ben.

"I hope this isn't how I die," said Gordon. "I always pictured myself dying on the field."

"This is a new kind of sport," said Shane. "Andromedan wrapping."

"Frederick," I yelled, "open the air lock doors in five . . . four . . . three . . . two . . . one . . ."

PSSSHOOOOOOT!

We were sucked out of the air lock by the vacuum of space, and flew directly toward hundreds of hungry Andromedans.

Battle for
the Moon

"Whoooooaaaa," I yelled, flying uncontrolledly through space.

"Don't forget your jetpack," said Shane. I looked over to see him come out of a spin with the perfect thrust.

But I was too dizzy to figure out how to do the same thing. Just before I spewed all over the inside of my helmet, I slammed into something squishy and came to a stop.

BLURB PLUP BLUUURP!

"Guys, I'm surrounded by three Andromedans!" I yelled.

Their vurp splattered all over my glass helmet as a

great green cloud formed around me. I tried to thrust away, but a tentacle wrapped itself around my leg, and I dragged it with me.

"Guys!" I screamed, but all I could hear from my friends were the same crazed screams I was giving off.

They were as terrified as I was.

I looked around to see more Andromedans than there were monsters, but the monsters were putting up a fight. Vampires with jetpacks flew around crazily, puncturing Andromedan heads with their sharp teeth and claws. Werewolves in space suits used their insane strength to pop the Andromedans' bulbous growths, sending green steam everywhere.

The vurping of my Andromedan was slowing down, and I could hear a deeper rumbling.

"No!" I yelled, knowing that the Andromedan was about to thunderburp. Suddenly remembering the membranium, I crawled up to the head of the Andromedan using its tentacle and whipped a membranium out of my belt. It opened its mouth wide, and I slammed the membranium down over its head. Just as the membranium sealed tight . . .

CRACK! POP!

The Andromedan thunderburped, blowing its own head apart and popping the membranium all over me in a spray of green goop.

"Gaaaah," I yelled as I cartwheeled backward.

I couldn't even tell what direction I was headed in. I was moving fast and getting faster by the second. If I didn't stop soon, I really would spew all over my helmet. As I spun, the moon came in and out of my view. I saw even more Andromedans on the moon—thousands— their heads pulsating as they drained it.

They got closer each time I saw them.

I was about to land in the center of them.

"Heeeeeeelp," I screeched.

In a flash, Shane grabbed me, and my spinning stopped.

"I gotcha, homey," he said.

"I'm so dizzy," I said. "My head aches. I think I popped an eardrum."

"Yeah, a nasty side effect of having to put the membranium on at the last minute," he said. "By the way, what happened to 'staying away from the battle'?"

"It wasn't my choice," I said.

I got my bearings and pushed off Shane. We rocketed away from the moon and back toward the battle. Above, monsters clashed with Andromedans, but except for the occasional thunderburp, it was completely silent. There was one large thunderburp, and another Andromedan popped, sending a monster flying toward the moon.

"Here," Shane said, handing me his membranium. "I'm going to get him."

He rocketed down, and I rocketed back up.

Most monsters had already run out of membranium and were now fighting with the tools they had left—fangs, claws, and jaws. I watched as Twenty-Three destroyed Andromedan after Andromedan, somehow able to push himself from one to the next with ease.

Two vampire bats flitted uncontrolledly past me. They must have lost their jetpacks when they transformed. I grabbed them and flung them back at a pair of Andromedans who were vurping all over a stunned Howie.

I saw Shane fling the monster he had caught back into the battle and rocket over to Gordon, Ben, and Nabila, who were in a tight circle. They were trying to collect the random body parts of monsters that had been thunderburped apart. Arms, legs, and heads floated everywhere.

I rocketed over to them.

"This doesn't look good," I said. "The monsters are getting destroyed, and—"

BEEP BEEP BEEP.

"What's that?" I asked.

A red light on Gordon's wrist was flashing, and we could hear an alarm inside our helmets.

"I don't know, but I'm having a hard time breathing," he said.

"Your oxygen is low," Director Z said over the intercom. "You need to get back on the ship as soon as you can. You only have a few minutes."

BEEP BEEP BEEP.

"Mine is low, too," said Nabila.

"We've got to get back to the ship!" I yelled.

"Correct you are," yelled a voice inside our helmets.

"Director Z?" I asked.

"No, it is I, Zorflogg, coming through on all frequencies," he said. "I've taken the liberty of listening in on your feeble attempt to destroy my beloved Andromedans, and I just can't take your whimpering anymore. You've already harmed too many of the most perfect creatures in the universe. You *do* have to get back to your ship. But that's going to be a little difficult if I blast it into atoms, isn't it?"

"Look!" Shane yelled, and he pointed to the moon's horizon.

A huge ship, with a jagged black spire on its nose, rocketed toward us. Behind it was a huge cloud of Andromedans—more than I had seen on the surface of the moon.

"Zorflogg," said Director Z, "leave these innocent children alone."

"Innocent children?" sneered Zorflogg. "There is nothing innocent about them, especially that sneaky yellow-haired one. I don't know how, but he got the pendant back. There's no other way to explain this madness. You never could have gotten these insane creatures into orbit without a pendant. But even a Director can suffocate. And so he shall."

Now all our suits were beeping. I looked behind me to see our ship in the distance. We were between it and Zorflogg's ship when the spire on the front of his ship glowed an ominous red, and—

ZAP!

A laser beam blasted our ship, blowing a chunk of metal off the back. Its tail pointed down toward the moon, and it began to fall.

"Noooooo!" I screamed. "Director Z!"

There was no reply.

Boom!

"What do we do?" asked Shane.

I knew I couldn't answer, or Zorflogg would hear. I turned off my radio and motioned to Shane to do the same. I pushed my glass helmet against his, hoping the sound would travel between the two.

"Our only hope is with Director Z and Frederick," I screamed. "We've got to keep the ship from falling into the moon's gravity and crash-landing. Hopefully they can give us that blast we're looking for."

It was no use, he couldn't hear me. I repeated myself, this time slowly and simpler, hoping that Shane could read my lips.

"How?" I thought he mouthed back.

"We get below the ship and thrust our jetpacks as hard as we can," I said, miming along. "We give Director Z as much time as we can."

Shane gave a thumbs-up.

I turned on my radio again.

"Everyone who can hear me," I yelled. "Follow me and bring the others with you. Do as I do!"

We thrust down to the ship. The monsters followed.

BEEP BEEP BEEP.

"I wish these suits would shut up," Gordon gasped.

"If they did, I think that means you'd be completely out of oxygen," I replied. "Everyone, try not to breathe heavy."

"Yeah, right," said Ben.

"Are you okay?" I radioed Director Z. "I don't care that Zorflogg can hear—just let me know you're alive."

Still nothing.

The Andromedans followed, vurping all the way.

First my friends and I arrived. We got under the tail of the ship and pushed on it as we thrust our jetpacks.

"Are we doing anything?" Gordon asked.

"Hard to tell," I said.

The monsters joined us, and the extra thrust helped. But soon the Andromedans arrived, and half the monsters had to fight them away from us. Soon, vurp filled the space around us, and I was worried that we'd soon be thunderburped into oblivion.

"Keep it up!" I yelled.

"Keep what up?" asked Zorflogg. "You really think you can keep the ship from falling? You fools! Stop this insolence."

The vurping suddenly stopped, but not because a thunderburp was about to happen. It was because Zorflogg's ship was only one hundred feet above us. The Andromedans scattered.

"Good news!" yelled Shane. "It's working!"

"Bad news!" I yelled. "We're about to get blasted. Everyone back off."

The monsters scattered. In the panic, everyone was bumping against one another to get out of the way. The nose of Zorflogg's ship glowed red and—

ZAP!

—blasted right between Gordon and me. Gordon went tumbling down toward the moon. Shane rocketed off to catch him. Monsters exploded from the heat. Howie's fur caught fire inside his suit.

"I've been hit," said Nabila. "I think my arm is burned. It hurts. My suit is okay."

"I'm coming," said Ben.

Through the radio, I could hear monsters moaning. Between the Andromedans and the last blast, our powered-up monsters had been nearly drained of their energy.

Suddenly, my suit stopped BEEPING. I could barely breathe.

"I don't think we're going to make it," I said to Shane.

"I disagree," he said, and pointed at the cable connecting the ship to the moon. It glowed a brilliant white-green.

"YES!" I screeched.

"Yes, what?" Zorflogg asked. "Answer me."

Up above, I could see the nose of our ship glow the same white-green.

It crackled like Frederick crackled when he had too much energy.

I was nearly breathless, but was able to say, "How's this for an answer?"

BLLLLLRRRRZZZZZZZT.

A great jagged ray of moon plasma erupted out of our ship and blasted Zorflogg's!

"Arrrggh, noooooooooo!" Zorflogg's voice came through static. "I can't believe I didn't crush you when I had the chance."

His ship fell past our ship and plummeted to the moon below.

"Eat moondust," Shane said, shaking his fist.

"This ship is designed to survive any crash, you little fool," said Zorflogg. "And in the meantime, my Andromedans will feast upon your measly bones."

"So we *are* doomed," said Ben, rocketing back with Nabila.

The Andromedans raced back, surrounding us with their vurps.

"I tried so hard," I said, wheezing.

"You did a good job, Boss," said Griselda. "I'm so proud of you, young man."

The monsters formed a tight protective circle around us, but it was no use.

"You guys are the best friends a space captain like me could ask for," I said, delirious.

"You're not half bad, yourself," said Shane.

"Is it okay if I cry a little?" asked Gordon.

"Please just shut up and die," said Zorflogg. "I . . . oh no! Aaaaaaaaah!"

"Look!" yelled Gordon, and he pointed down at the surface of the moon.

The Andromedans stopped vurping for a moment.

A huge grinning mouth had appeared on the moon's craggy surface, and as Zorflogg's ship got closer, it opened wide, and a massive tongue curled out of it.

Zorflogg's ship crash-landed on the tongue and bounced deeper into the mouth.

"Noooooooo—" Zorflogg's scream was cut off, and over the intercom, we could hear CRUNCH MUNCH MUNCH.

The mouth drooled slightly as the moon enjoyed its snack.

Thousands of Andromedans, enraged, vurped once

more, ready to destroy us, but suddenly—

BRRRRAAAAAAAAPPPPPPPP!

The moon burped the loudest burp in the universe. It blasted right past us and all the monsters, instantly shattering the heads of the thousands of Andromedans. A white-green haze floated down to the moon. North of the mouth, a nose exploded from the ground, and two nostrils the size of Rhode Island breathed in deeply.

SNNNNIIIIIIIIFFFFFF.

A great laugh shook our space suits.

But I was too weak to laugh.

"Need," I said. "Ship. Need. Air."

My fingers slipped off my jetpack controls. But I felt someone—maybe it was Shane, maybe it was one of the monsters—guide me back to the cargo hold of the ship.

We floated for another moment in silence, and then there was a hiss of oxygen as the room filled with air.

But it was too late.

I blacked out . . .

. . . only to be awoken by Grigore.

"Don't give up, Boss," he said, and slapped me across the face.

"HWWWAAAAAH!"

I breathed for what felt like the first time in my life. White light exploded in my head. I looked around to see everyone else gasping as well. Nabila moaned in pain as Griselda tended to her burn. Gordon threw up so hard that he began doing cartwheels in the room. Some monsters had been reduced to parts. Twenty-Three appeared limp and lifeless. Camilla floated past me in freeze-dried vampire bat form—doomed to be stuck in that shape for all eternity like some sort of bat jerky.

"I hope it was worth it," I said.

"Oh, it was worth it," Director Z said, floating over to me. "You've saved the moon, monsterdom, and the entire human race."

"I know," I said. "But I've lost so many friends."

"Your friends are fine," said Director Z. "They just need a little R & R. They'll be on the right track in no time."

"No, I mean all my monster friends," I said. "Look at them. They're more beat-up than I've ever seen them. The ones that are left, anyway."

I floated over to Howie, whose fur was burned off completely. He shivered in the cold cargo hold, his body twitching violently.

"Oh, Howie," I said, trying to comfort him.

"Hoooooooowl," Howie howled weakly.

Below us, at the point where the cable from the moon was connected to our ship, the metal glowed a brilliant white-green.

The same plasma that had shot out of the nose of the ship now connected with every single one of the monsters. Their eyes became bright, and they puffed out their chests. The chunks of leftover monsters pieced themselves together to re-form monsters that we thought were lost.

"Wow," said Shane. "The power of the moon."

With a brilliant flash, the light was gone.

And many of my monster friends were back and better than before.

"YIPPPEEEE!" everyone cheered.

Monsters hugged monsters. Kids hugged monsters. Kids hugged kids. Some kids kissed other kids.

"Ew, stop it, Ben!" said Nabila.

"Sorry, I couldn't help it," Ben said.

"Hey, Boss!" Grigore said, floating over.

"Grigore, you look amazing!" I said, and awkwardly hugged him. "Black hair! Not one wrinkle!"

"Yeah, and not jacked up on monster juice, either," said Shane. "That was pretty freaky!"

Grigore ended the hug and handed me a bloodstone on a gold chain. "You almost lost your pendant," he said.

"This isn't mine," I said.

"If this isn't yours, then vhere is yours?" Grigore asked, confused.

"We Directors always have something up our sleeves," I answered. "Don't we, Director Z?"

I placed the pendant over his head.

"You're BACK," yelled Shane, and high-fived Director Z.

"Thanks to Chris," said Director Z, "we're all back."

Headed Home

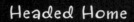

We landed our ship back on the moon and quickly made repairs. We searched for the ship that Murrayhotep had taken to the moon. Once we found it, Director Z put the coordinates for our town into the system.

"There," he said. "Now you'll be able to sit back, relax, and enjoy the ride."

"Are you sure one of us shouldn't come back with you on the Victorian scientist's ship?" I asked.

"Well, now that I have this back," he said, touching the bloodstone necklace hidden under his suit, "I shouldn't have too much of a problem. Plus, that old ship is so rickety and unreliable that it's only suitable for monsters."

"I wish we could stick around a little longer," Gordon said. "I was really looking forward to playing football on the moon."

"Well, I suppose we could stay," said Director Z. "But not too much longer. It's getting hard to keep track of all the lies we're telling your parents, and there could be more Andromedans on the way. The new ones wouldn't know how to drain the moon, but they would probably be quite upset that their friends are no longer here. I wouldn't want to be here to witness their anger."

So we played football on the moon, with Shane and me leading a team of vampires and zombies, and Gordon, Nabila, and Ben leading a team of werewolves and banshees. My team won 24–14. Gordon blamed his space suit, but I think he just didn't have a good grasp of how to use the gravity and lack of air to his advantage.

"I can't believe I have to tell everyone back home that I lost a football game to you!" said Gordon. "Are you *sure* I can't mention we were playing on the moon?"

"It would probably be best if we kept that secret," I said.

We stood in front of Murrayhotep's ship, the monsters in front of us proudly waving good-bye.

"Thank you!" Grigore yelled, and he flashed his sharp fangs with joy.

"Get home safe!" yelled Jill.

"Howl if you need us," said Howie.

"It's so good to see them so strong," said Shane as we stepped on board.

"I know," I said. "Now they really don't need us anymore."

"I wonder, if they don't need us, are they going to eat us now?" asked Ben. "I always worry about that."

"We know," said Nabila. "But there's the Code of Monsterdom."

"Oh right," Ben said. "But these guys haven't had anything good to eat since—"

"Stop it!" we yelled.

After takeoff, I floated next to the window with Shane, sad to see the moon getting smaller.

"You still have your telescope," Shane said.

"I guess," I said. "But after having been on the surface, even underneath it—literally, inside it—it won't ever be the same."

"I'm sure we'll make it back one day," said Shane. "It's safe now that Zorflogg's gone."

"And good riddance," I said. "That guy was terrible."

"And his breath was insanely bad!" said Gordon.

"The only person in the universe with worse breath than Mr. Bradley," said Ben.

We all laughed.

"It was all the monster juice," Nabila said, laughing harder.

We laughed until we snorted, and then Shane and

I looked out our window, this time at the blue ball that was getting larger.

"Hey," Shane broke the silence. "I wonder what ever happened to Murrayhotep."

About the author . . .

M. D. Payne is a mad scientist who creates monsters by stitching together words instead of dead body parts. After nearly a decade in multimedia production for public radio, he entered children's publishing as a copywriter and marketer. Monster Juice is his debut series. He lives in the tiny village of New York City with his wife and baby girl, and hopes to add a hairy, four-legged monster to his family soon.